AVENGERS K #5
THE ADVENT OF ULTRON

JIM ZUB
SCRIPT

WOO BIN CHOI with **JAE SUNG LEE**
PENCILS

MIN JU LEE
INKS

JAE WOONG LEE
COLORS

VC's CORY PETIT
LETTERS

WOO BIN CHOI with **JAE SUNG LEE, MIN JU LEE** & **JAE WOONG LEE**
COVER ART

AVENGERS VS. ULTRON is adapted from AVENGERS ORIGINS: SCARLET WITCH & QUICKSILVER #1,
AVENGERS ORIGINS: ANT-MAN & THE WASP #1, and AVENGERS (1963) #57.
Adaptations written by SI YEON PARK and translated by JI EUN PARK

AVENGERS created by STAN LEE and JACK KIRBY

Original comics written by SEAN McKEEVER, ROBERTO AGUIRRE-SACASA, and ROY THOMAS;
and illustrated by MIRCO PIERFEDERICI, STEPHANIE HANS, and JOHN BUSCEMA

Editor SARAH BRUNSTAD
Manager, Licensed Publishing JEFF REINGOLD
VP, Brand Management & Development, Asia C.B. CEBULSKI
VP, Production & Special Projects JEFF YOUNGQUIST
SVP Print, Sales & Marketing DAVID GABRIEL
Associate Manager, Digital Assets JOE HOCHSTEIN
Associate Managing Editor ALEX STARBUCK
Senior Editor, Special Projects JENNIFER GRÜNWALD
Editor, Special Projects MARK D. BEAZLEY
Book Designer ADAM DEL RE

Editor In Chief AXEL ALONSO
Chief Creative Officer JOE QUESADA
President DAN BUCKLEY
Executive Producer ALAN FINE

ABDO
Spotlight

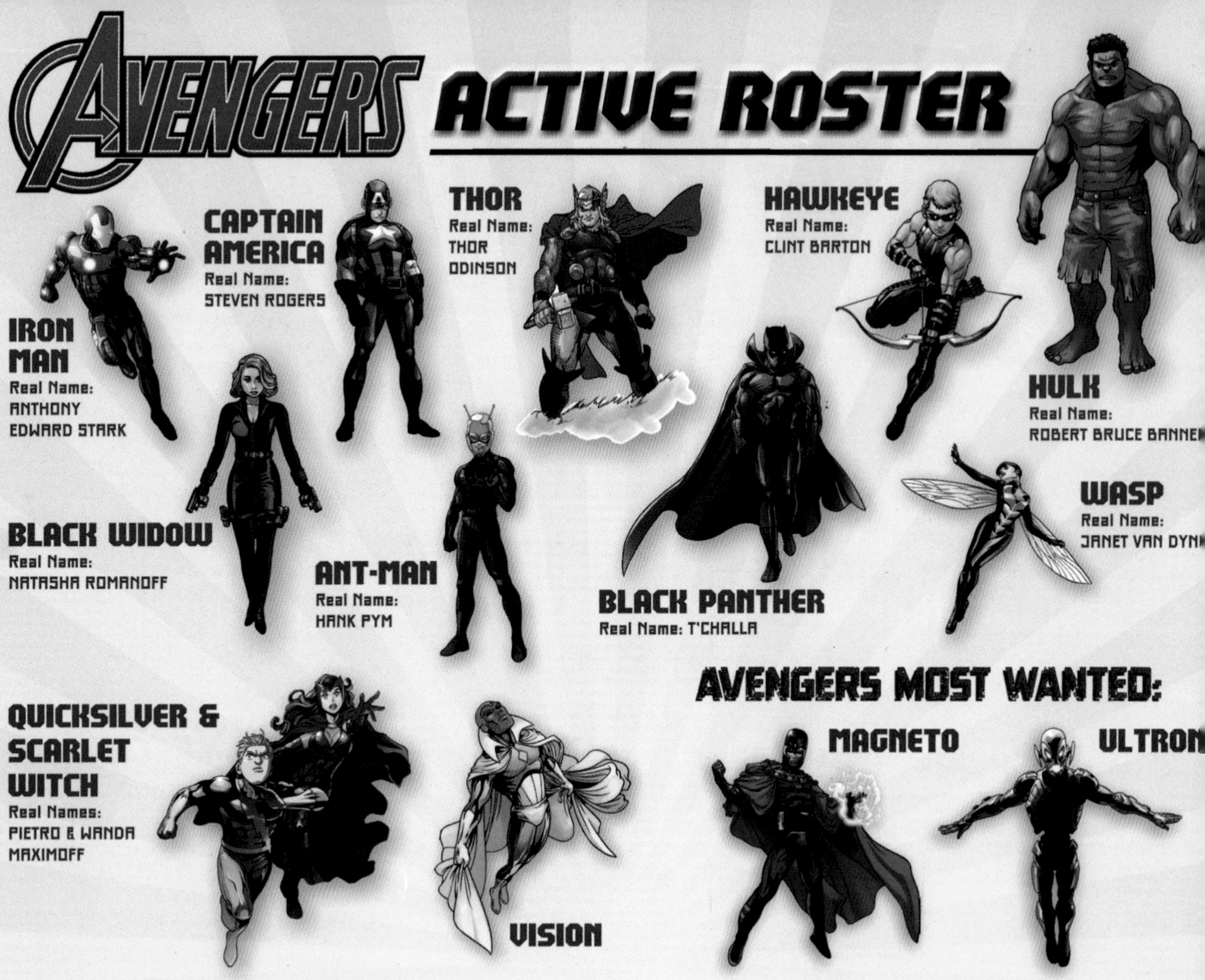

AVENGERS
ACTIVE ROSTER
IRON MAN
Real Name:
ANTHONY EDWARD STARK
CAPTAIN AMERICA
Real Name:
STEVEN ROGERS
THOR
Real Name:
THOR ODINSON
HAWKEYE
Real Name:
CLINT BARTON
HULK
Real Name:
ROBERT BRUCE BANNER
BLACK WIDOW
Real Name:
NATASHA ROMANOFF
ANT-MAN
Real Name:
HANK PYM
BLACK PANTHER
Real Name: T'CHALLA
WASP
Real Name:
JANET VAN DYNE
QUICKSILVER & SCARLET WITCH
Real Names:
PIETRO & WANDA MAXIMOFF
VISION
AVENGERS MOST WANTED:
MAGNETO
ULTRON

ABDOPUBLISHING.COM

Reinforced library bound edition published in 2018 by Spotlight, a division of ABDO, PO Box 398166, Minneapolis, Minnesota 55439.
Spotlight produces high-quality reinforced library bound editions for schools and libraries. Published by agreement with Marvel Characters, Inc.
Printed in the United States of America, North Mankato, Minnesota.
042017 092017

MARVEL
marvelkids.com

THIS BOOK CONTAINS RECYCLED MATERIALS

PUBLISHER'S CATALOGING IN PUBLICATION DATA

Names: Zub, Jim, author. | Choi, Woo Bin ; Lee, Jae Sung ; Lee, Min Ju ; Lee, Jae Woong, illustrators.
Title: The advent of Ultron / writer: Jim Zub ; art: Woo Bin Choi ; Jae Sung Lee ; Min Ju Lee ; Jae Woong Lee.
Description: Reinforced library bound edition. | Minneapolis, Minnesota : Spotlight, 2018. | Series: Avengers K Set 2
Summary: Learn about the beginnings of your favorite Avengers, including Quicksilver and the Scarlet Witch's time with Magneto, how Ant-Man and the Wasp became a team, and the Vision's struggle to understand where he came from.
Identifiers: LCCN 2016961923 | ISBN 9781532140013 (v.1 ; lib. bdg.) | ISBN 9781532140020 (v.2 ; lib. bdg.) | ISBN 9781532140037 (v.3 ; lib. bdg.) | ISBN 9781532140044 (v.4 ; lib. bdg.) | ISBN 9781532140051 (v.5 ; lib. bdg.) | ISBN 9781532140068 (v.6 ; lib. bdg.)
Subjects: LCSH: Avengers (Fictitious characters)--Juvenile fiction. | Adventure and adventurers--Juvenile fiction. | Comic books, strips, etc.--Juvenile fiction. | Graphic novels--Juvenile fiction.
Classification: DDC 741.5--dc23
LC record available at https://lccn.loc.gov/2016961923

ABDO
Spotlight

A Division of ABDO
abdopublishing.com

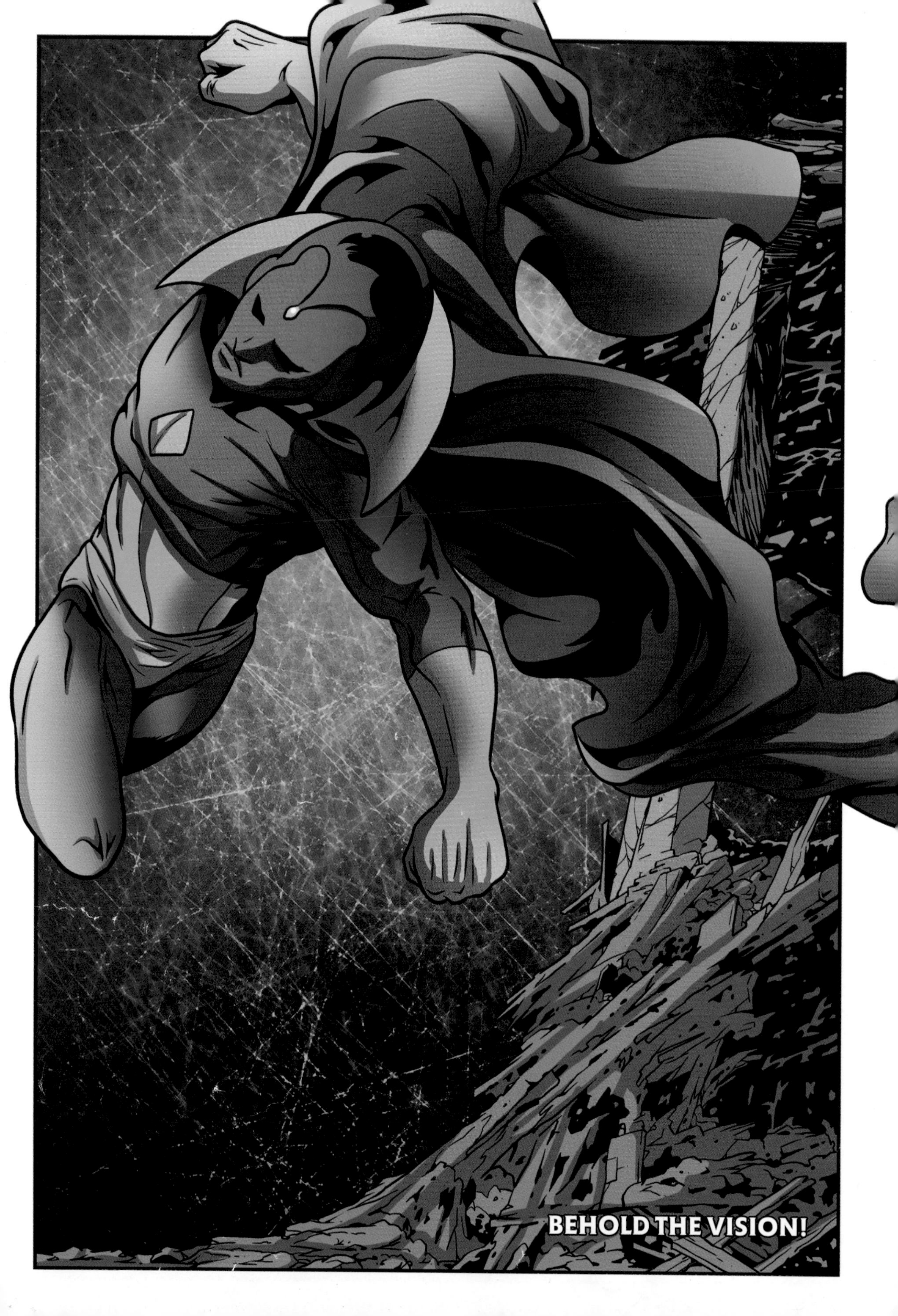
BEHOLD THE VISION!

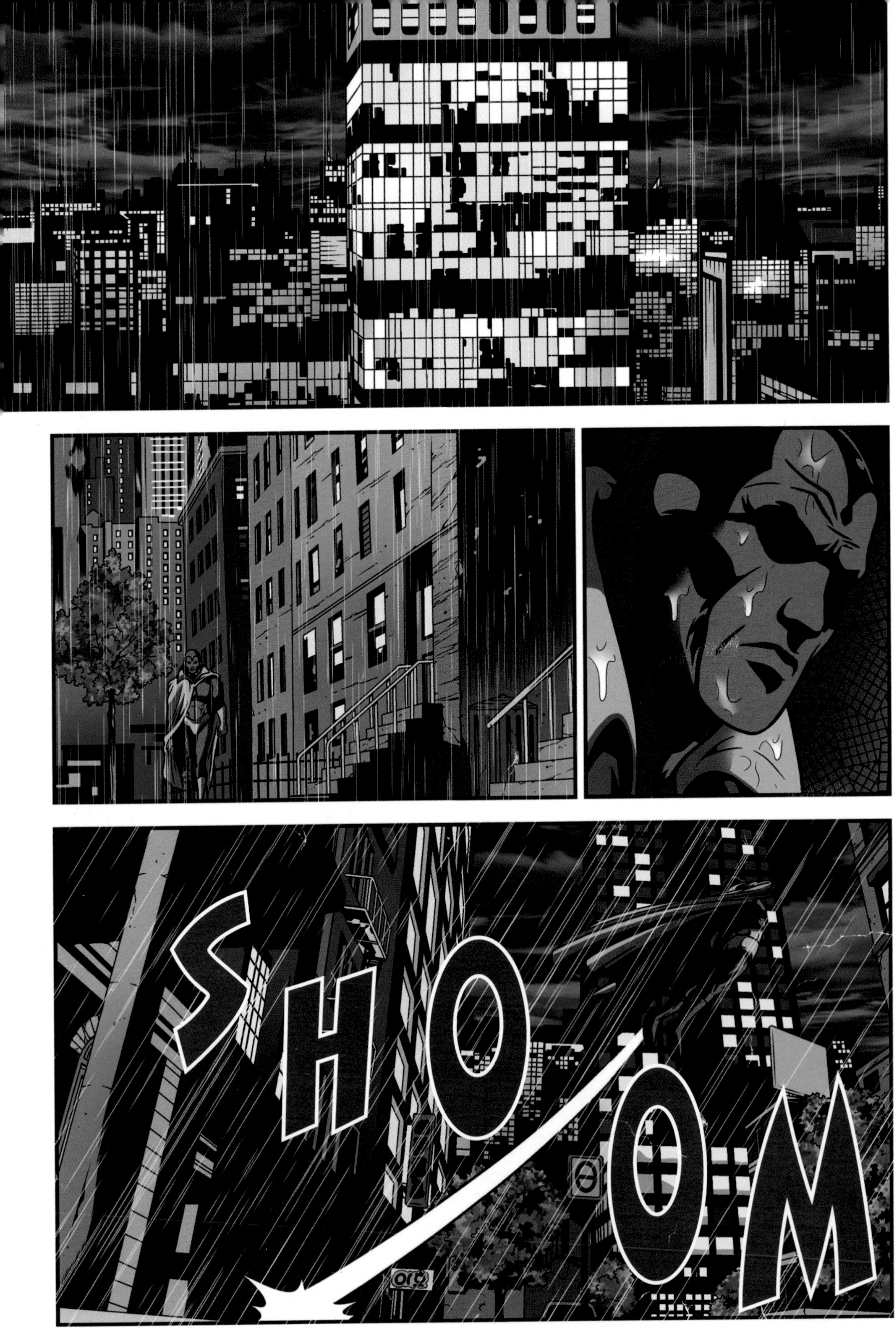
SHOOM

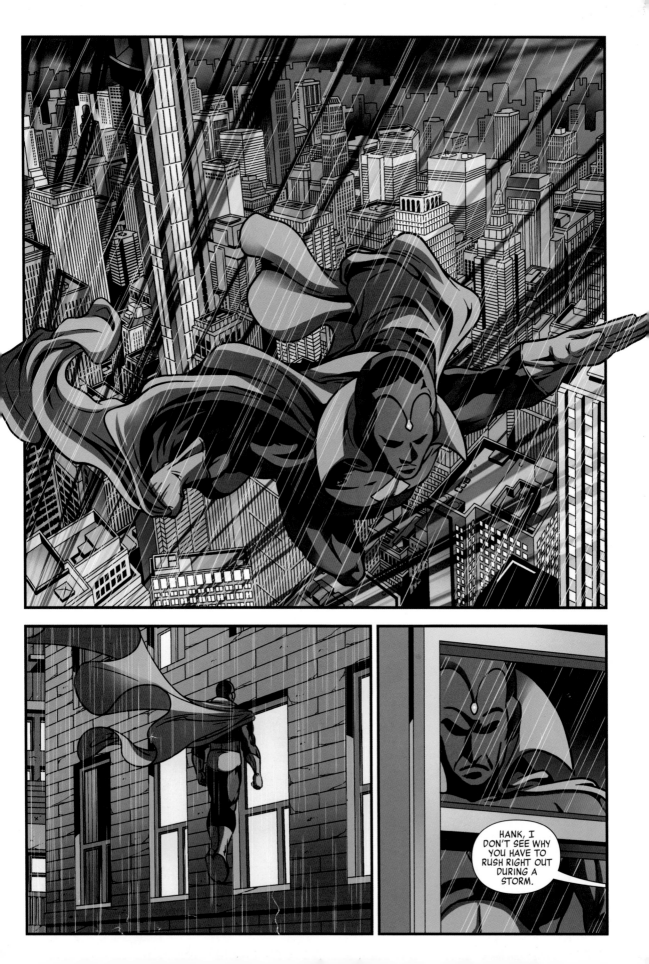

HANK, I DON'T SEE WHY YOU HAVE TO RUSH RIGHT OUT DURING A STORM.

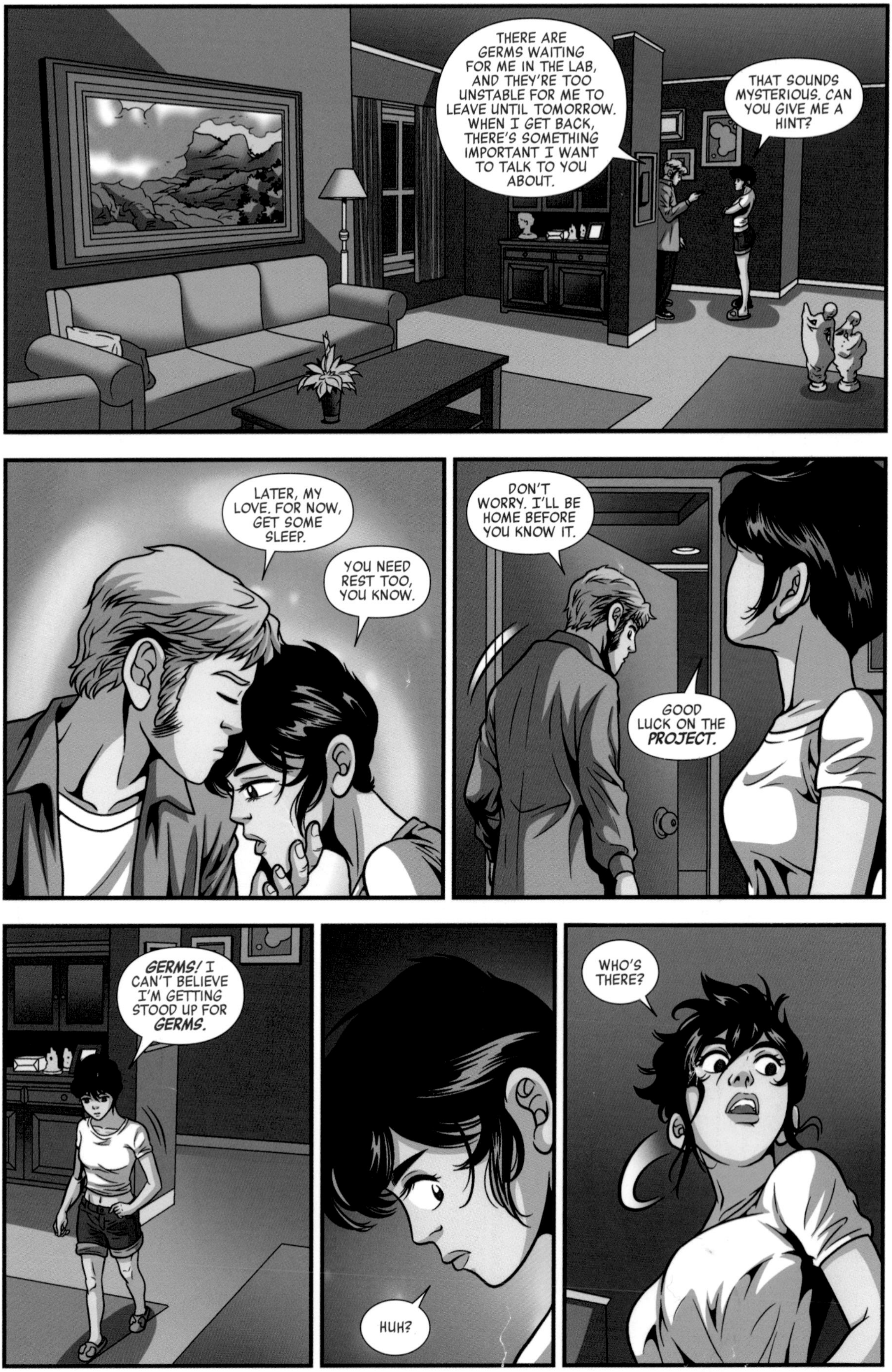
THERE ARE GERMS WAITING FOR ME IN THE LAB, AND THEY'RE TOO UNSTABLE FOR ME TO LEAVE UNTIL TOMORROW. WHEN I GET BACK, THERE'S SOMETHING IMPORTANT I WANT TO TALK TO YOU ABOUT.
THAT SOUNDS MYSTERIOUS. CAN YOU GIVE ME A HINT?
LATER, MY LOVE. FOR NOW, GET SOME SLEEP.
YOU NEED REST TOO, YOU KNOW.
DON'T WORRY. I'LL BE HOME BEFORE YOU KNOW IT.
GOOD LUCK ON THE PROJECT.
GERMS! I CAN'T BELIEVE I'M GETTING STOOD UP FOR GERMS.
HUH?
WHO'S THERE?

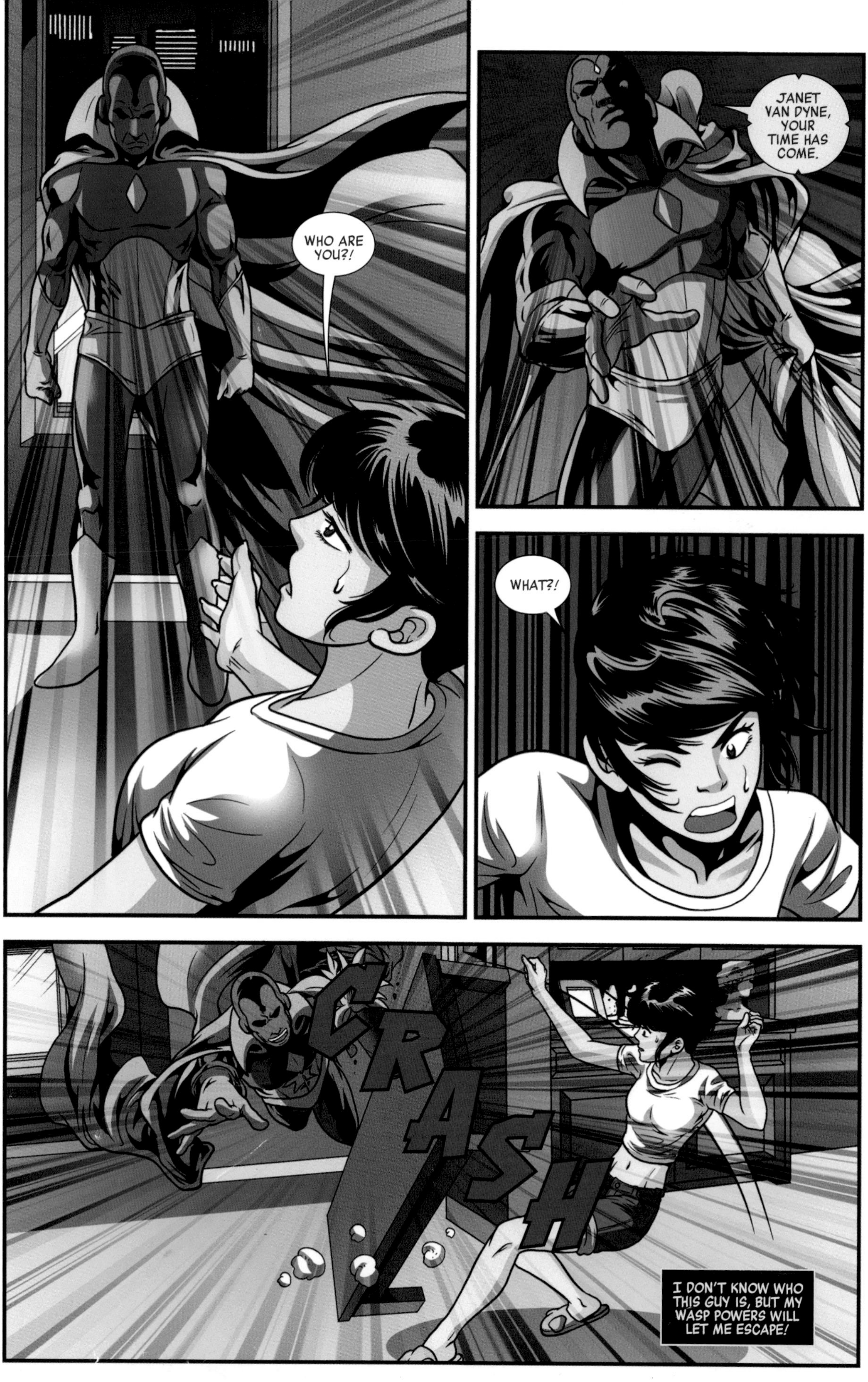
WHO ARE YOU?!
JANET VAN DYNE, YOUR TIME HAS COME.
WHAT?!
CRASH
I DON'T KNOW WHO THIS GUY IS, BUT MY WASP POWERS WILL LET ME ESCAPE!

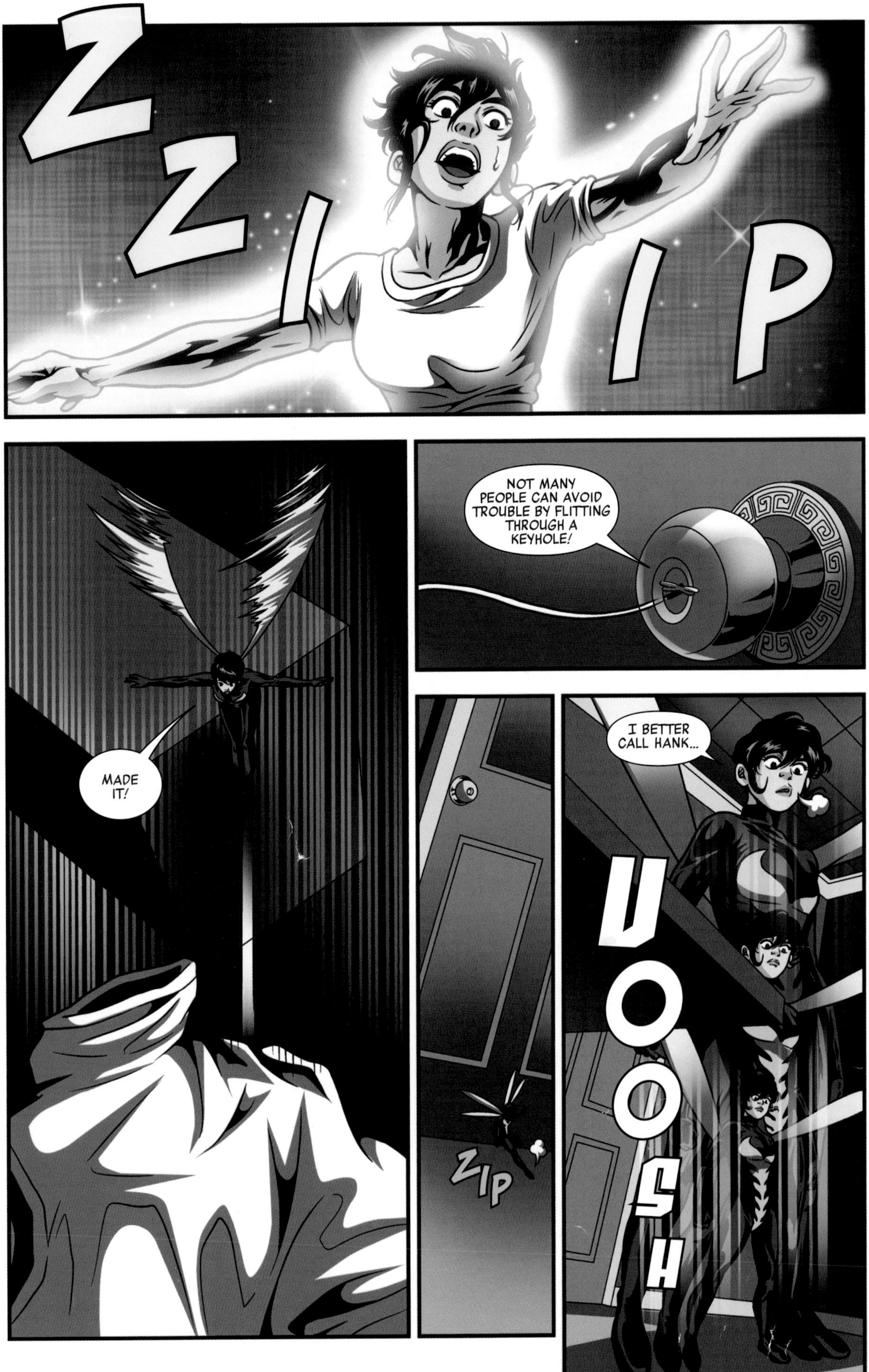
ZZIIP
NOT MANY PEOPLE CAN AVOID TROUBLE BY FLITTING THROUGH A KEYHOLE!
MADE IT!
ZIP
I BETTER CALL HANK...
VOOOSH

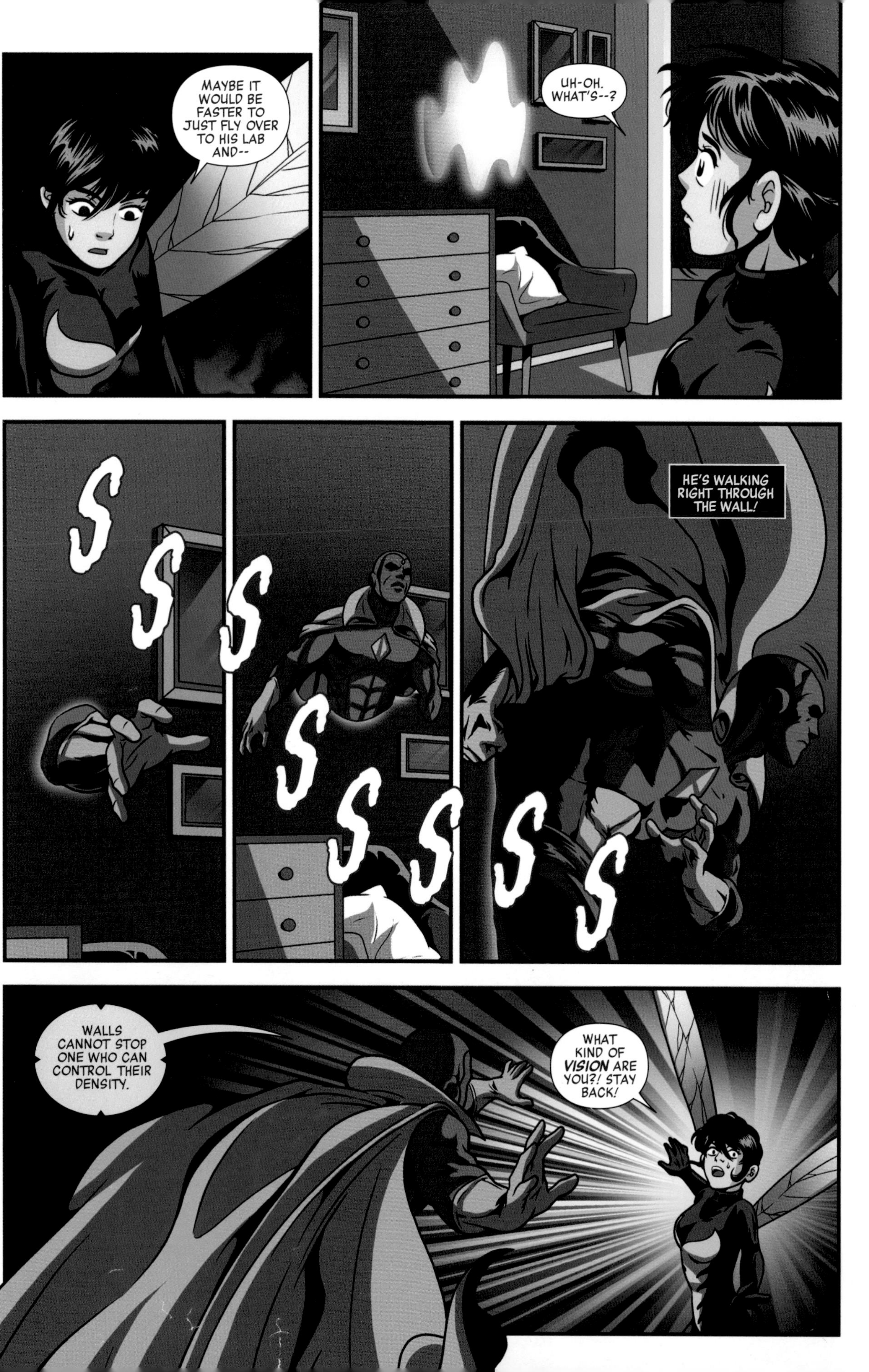
MAYBE IT WOULD BE FASTER TO JUST FLY OVER TO HIS LAB AND--
UH-OH. WHAT'S--?
SSSSSSSSSS
HE'S WALKING RIGHT THROUGH THE WALL!
WALLS CANNOT STOP ONE WHO CAN CONTROL THEIR DENSITY.
WHAT KIND OF VISION ARE YOU?! STAY BACK!

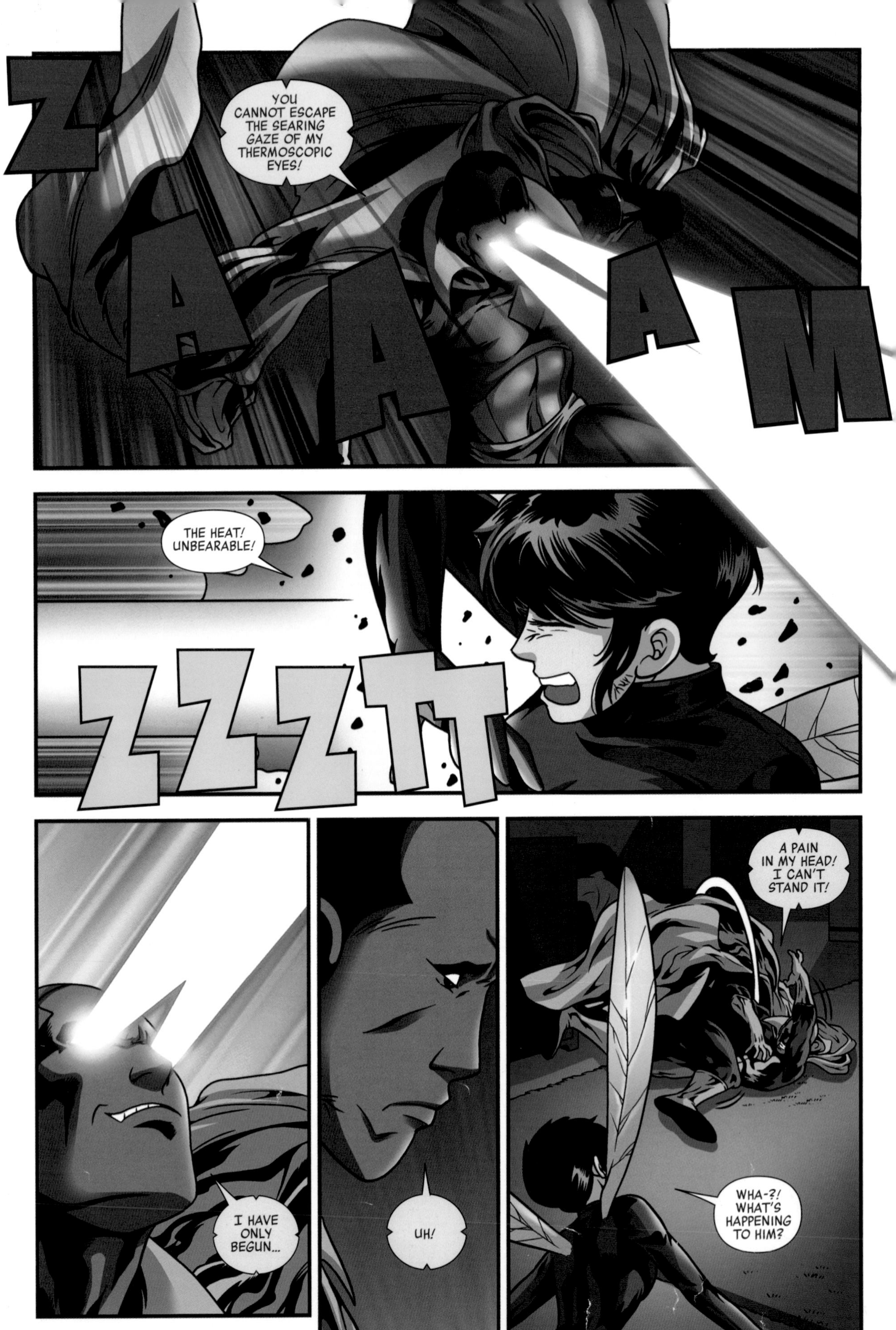
YOU CANNOT ESCAPE THE SEARING GAZE OF MY THERMOSCOPIC EYES!
ZZAAAM
THE HEAT! UNBEARABLE!
ZZZTT
I HAVE ONLY BEGUN...
UH!
A PAIN IN MY HEAD! I CAN'T STAND IT!
WHA-?! WHAT'S HAPPENING TO HIM?

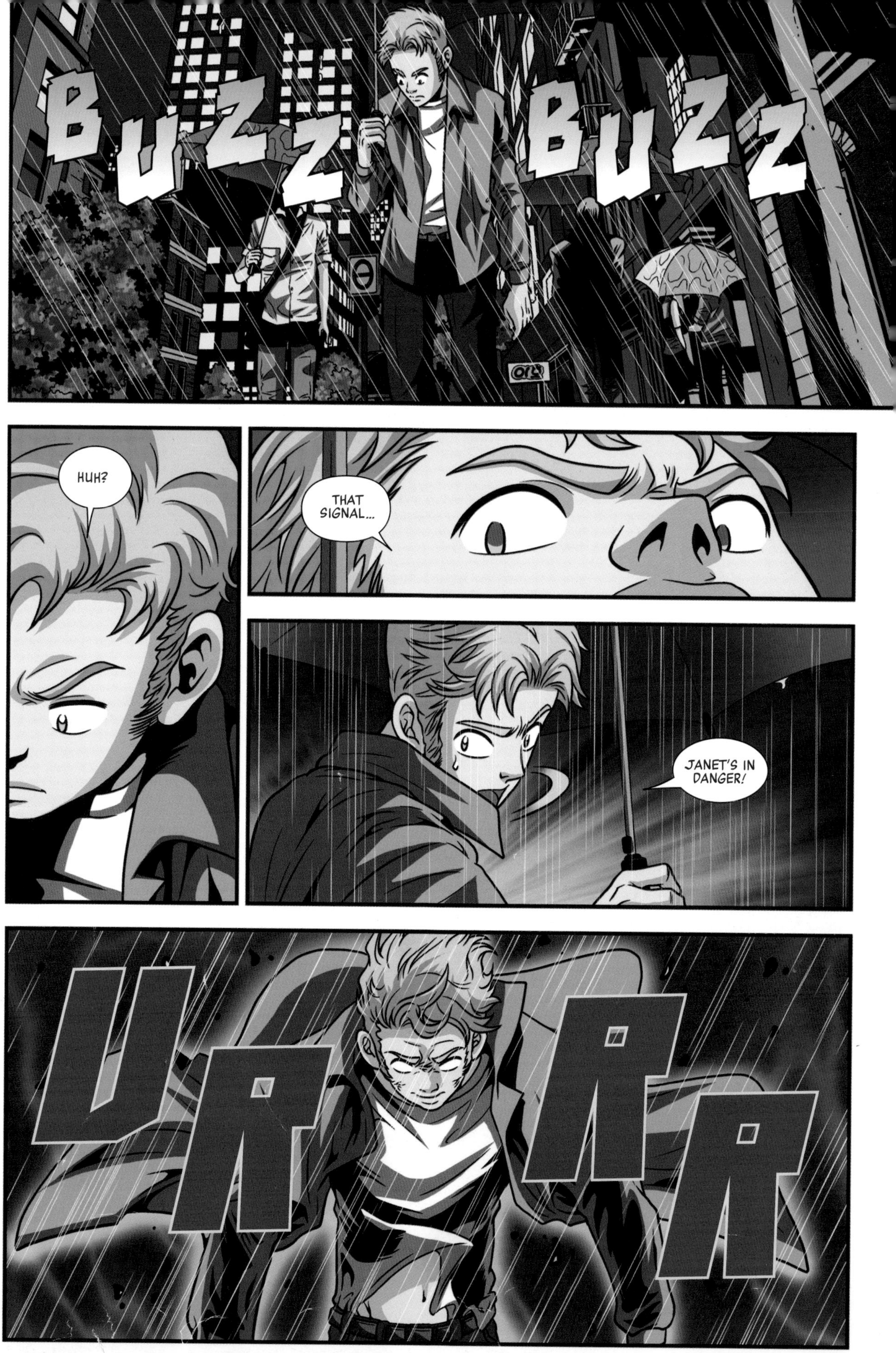
BUZZ BUZZ
HUH?
THAT SIGNAL...
JANET'S IN DANGER!
URRR

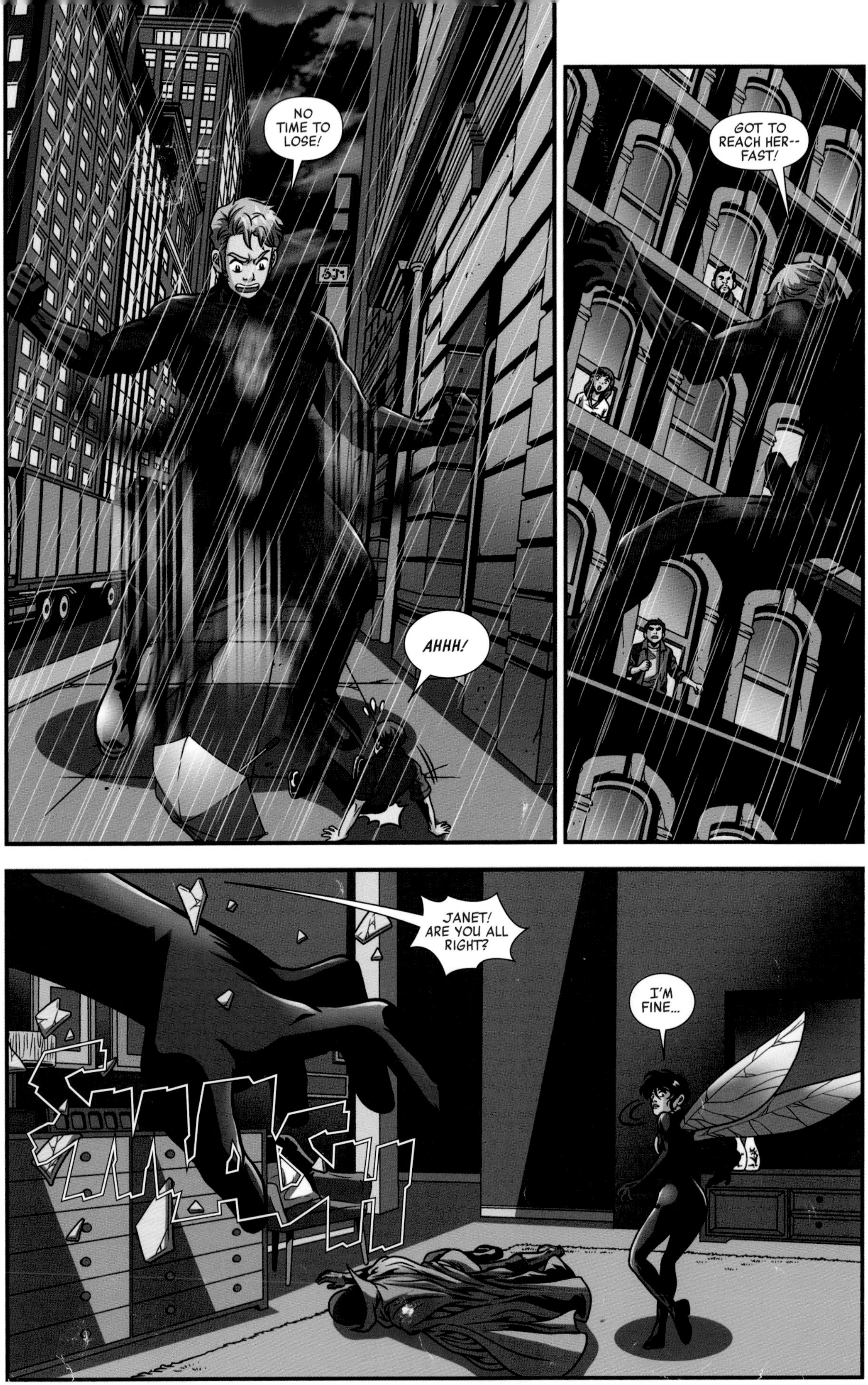
NO TIME TO LOSE!
AHHH!
GOT TO REACH HER-- FAST!
JANET! ARE YOU ALL RIGHT?
I'M FINE...

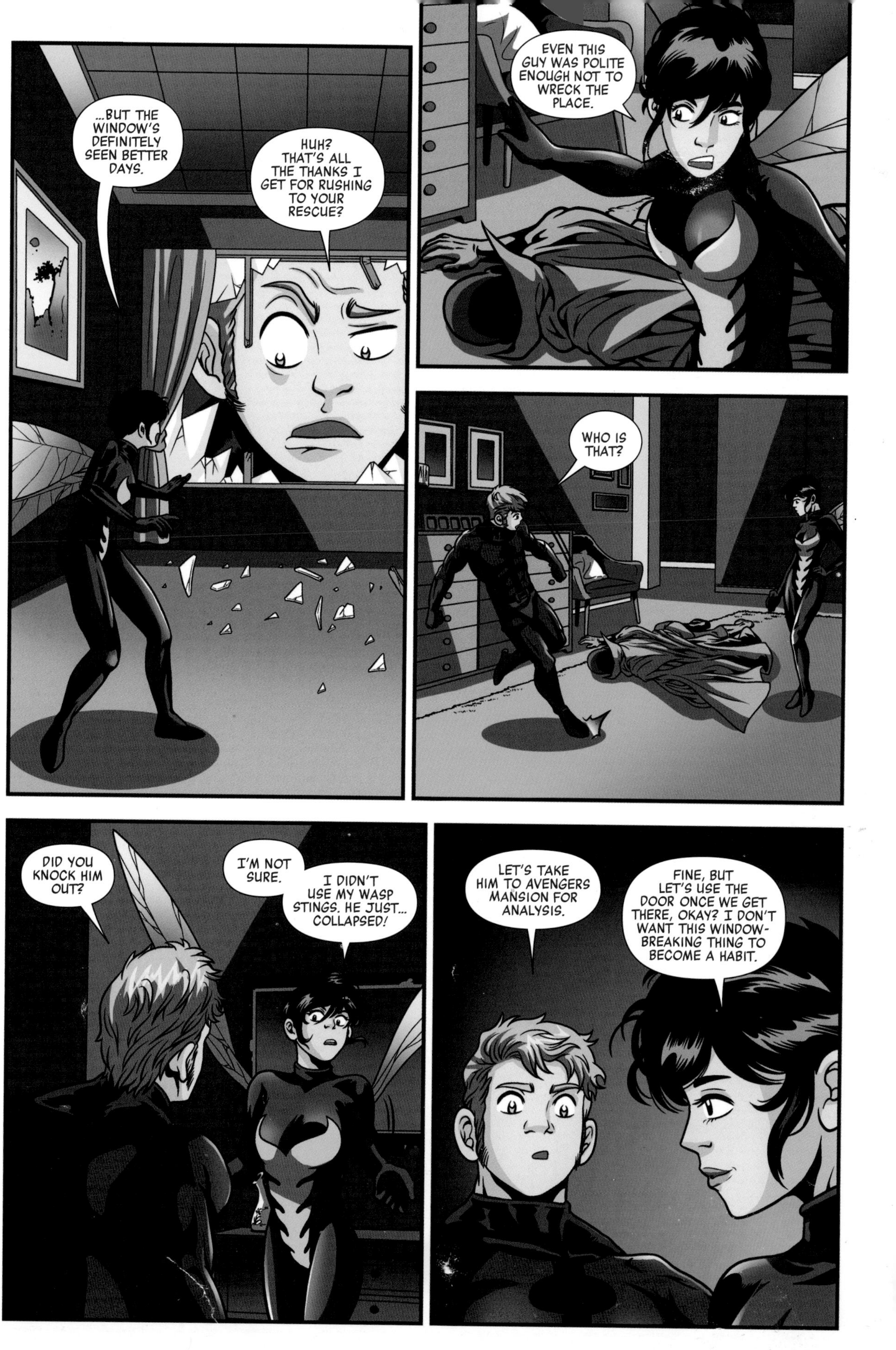
...BUT THE WINDOW'S DEFINITELY SEEN BETTER DAYS.
HUH? THAT'S ALL THE THANKS I GET FOR RUSHING TO YOUR RESCUE?
EVEN THIS GUY WAS POLITE ENOUGH NOT TO WRECK THE PLACE.
WHO IS THAT?
DID YOU KNOCK HIM OUT?
I'M NOT SURE.
I DIDN'T USE MY WASP STINGS. HE JUST... COLLAPSED!
LET'S TAKE HIM TO AVENGERS MANSION FOR ANALYSIS.
FINE, BUT LET'S USE THE DOOR ONCE WE GET THERE, OKAY? I DON'T WANT THIS WINDOW-BREAKING THING TO BECOME A HABIT.

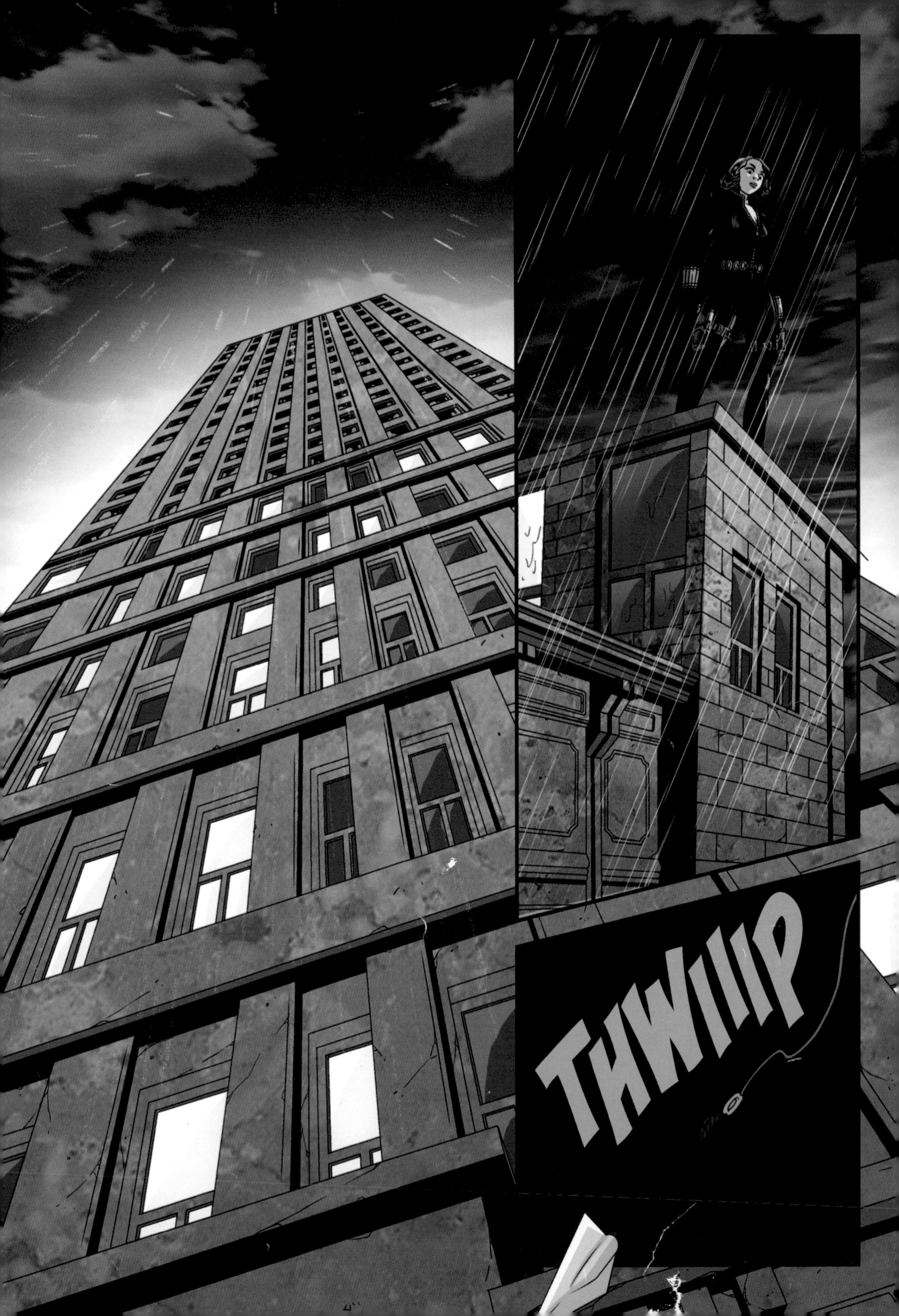
THWIIIP

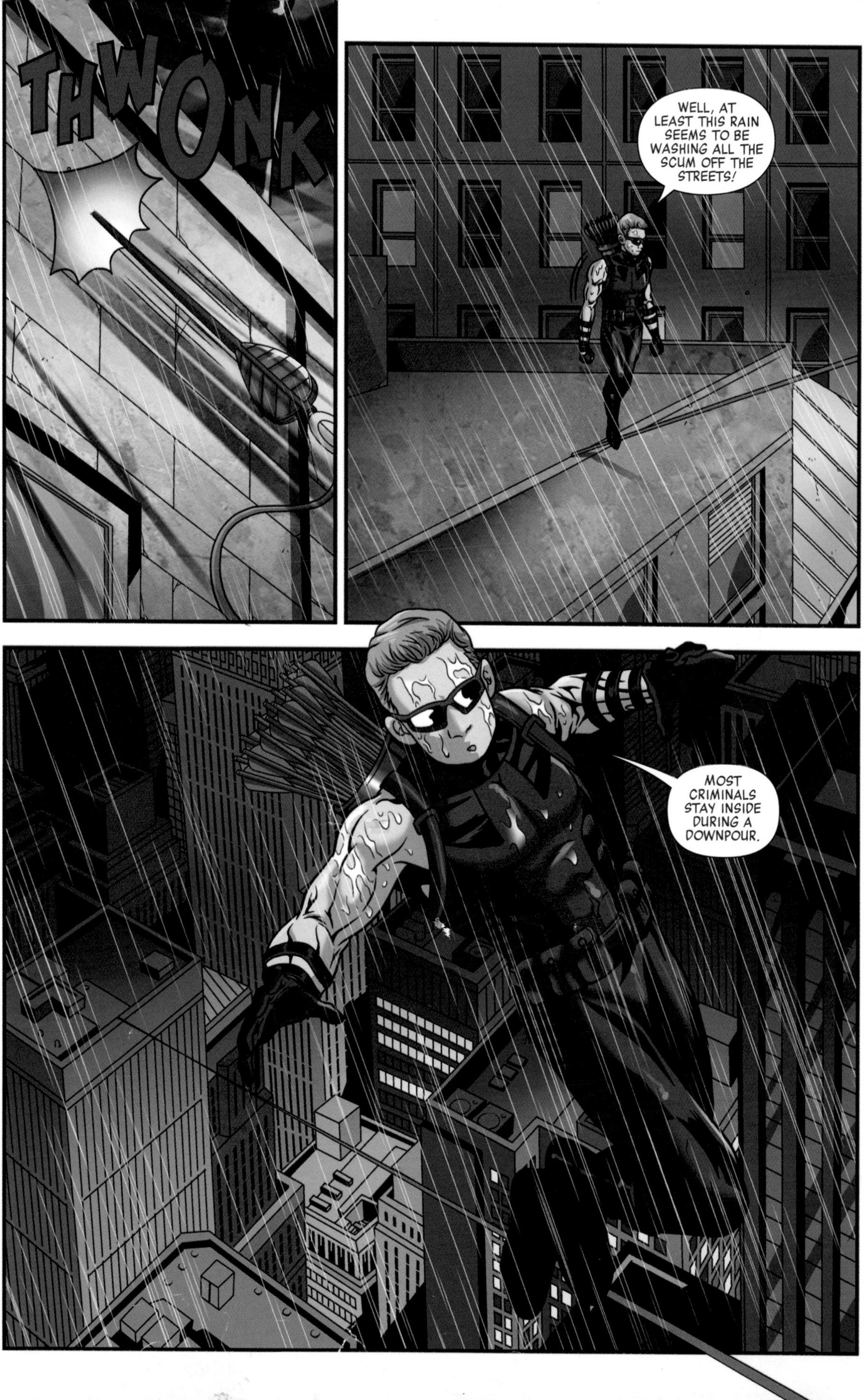
THWONK
WELL, AT LEAST THIS RAIN SEEMS TO BE WASHING ALL THE SCUM OFF THE STREETS!
MOST CRIMINALS STAY INSIDE DURING A DOWNPOUR.

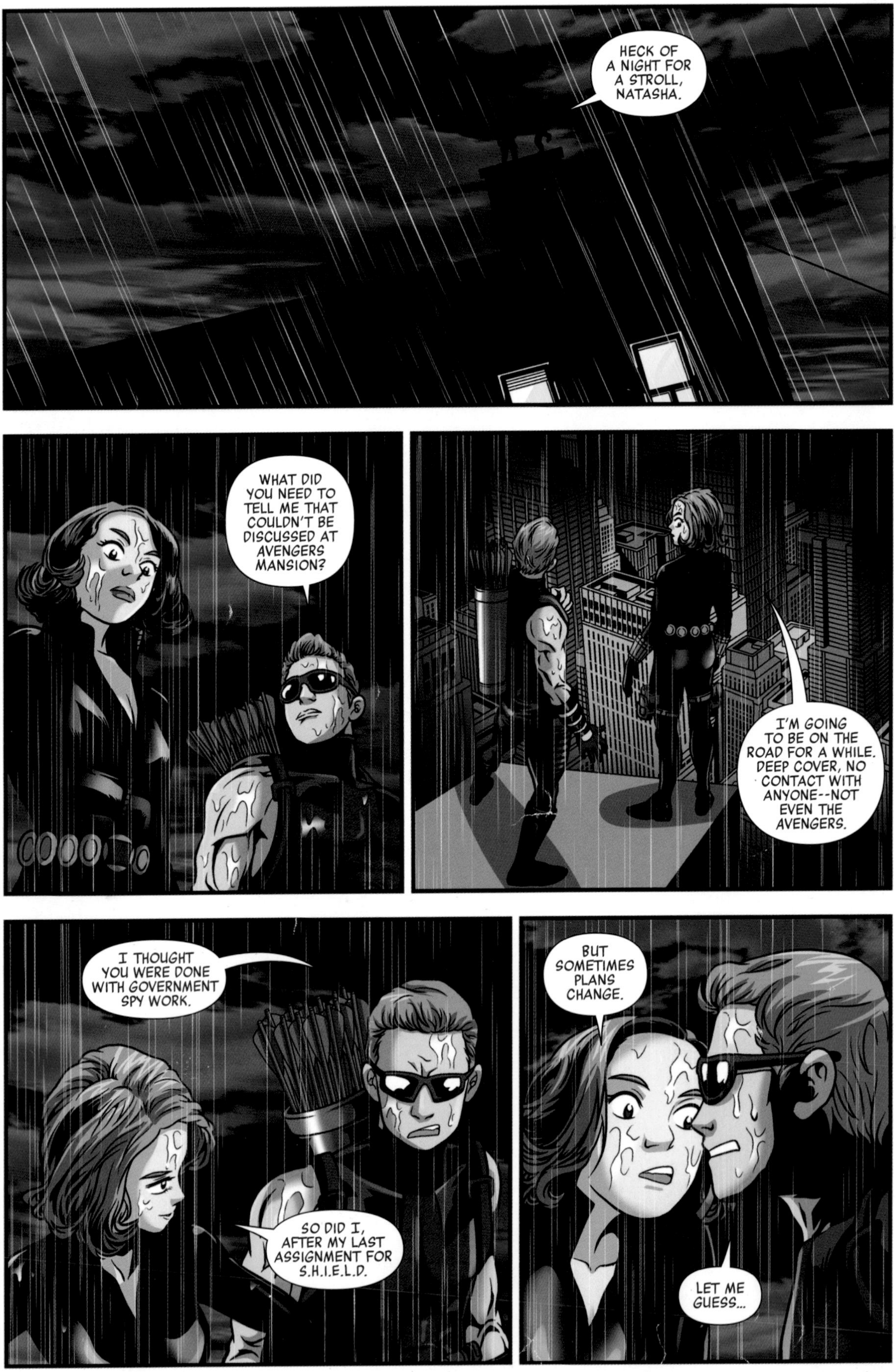
HECK OF A NIGHT FOR A STROLL, NATASHA.
WHAT DID YOU NEED TO TELL ME THAT COULDN'T BE DISCUSSED AT AVENGERS MANSION?
I'M GOING TO BE ON THE ROAD FOR A WHILE. DEEP COVER, NO CONTACT WITH ANYONE--NOT EVEN THE AVENGERS.
I THOUGHT YOU WERE DONE WITH GOVERNMENT SPY WORK.
SO DID I, AFTER MY LAST ASSIGNMENT FOR S.H.I.E.L.D.
BUT SOMETIMES PLANS CHANGE.
LET ME GUESS...

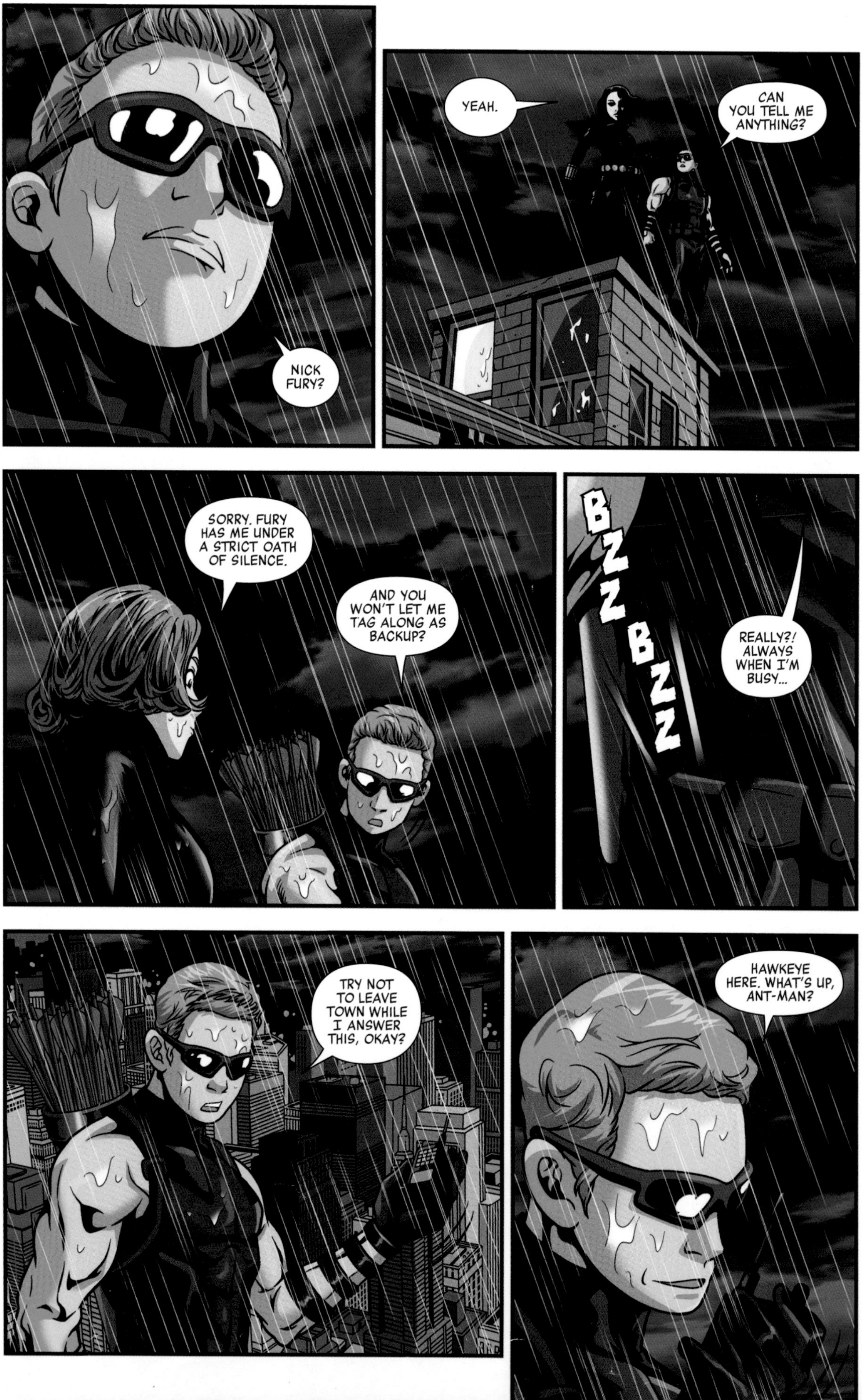
NICK FURY?
CAN YOU TELL ME ANYTHING?
YEAH.
SORRY. FURY HAS ME UNDER A STRICT OATH OF SILENCE.
AND YOU WON'T LET ME TAG ALONG AS BACKUP?
BZZ BZZ
REALLY?! ALWAYS WHEN I'M BUSY...
TRY NOT TO LEAVE TOWN WHILE I ANSWER THIS, OKAY?
HAWKEYE HERE. WHAT'S UP, ANT-MAN?

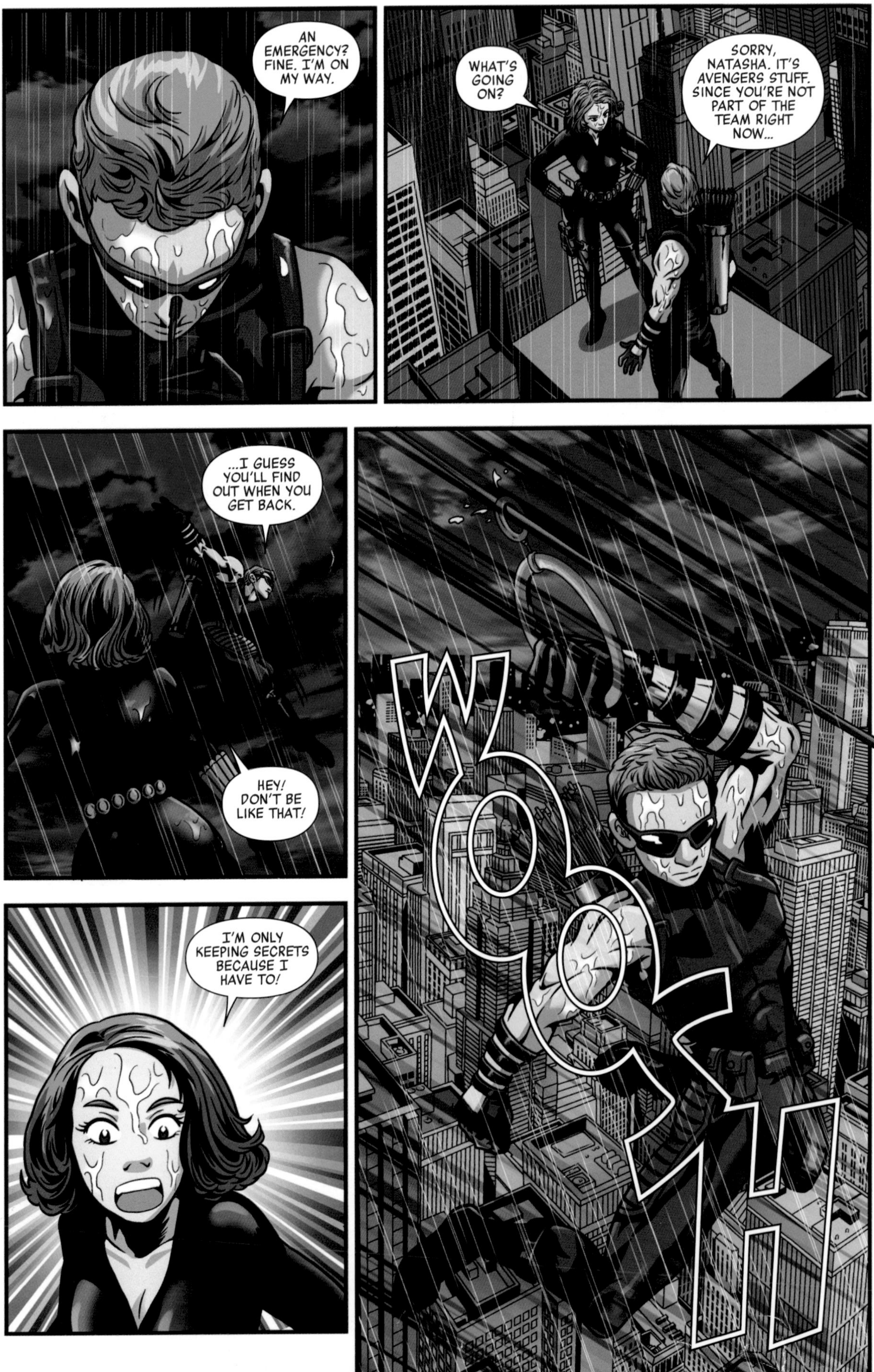
AN EMERGENCY? FINE. I'M ON MY WAY.
WHAT'S GOING ON?
SORRY, NATASHA. IT'S AVENGERS STUFF. SINCE YOU'RE NOT PART OF THE TEAM RIGHT NOW...
...I GUESS YOU'LL FIND OUT WHEN YOU GET BACK.
HEY! DON'T BE LIKE THAT!
I'M ONLY KEEPING SECRETS BECAUSE I HAVE TO!
WOOOSH

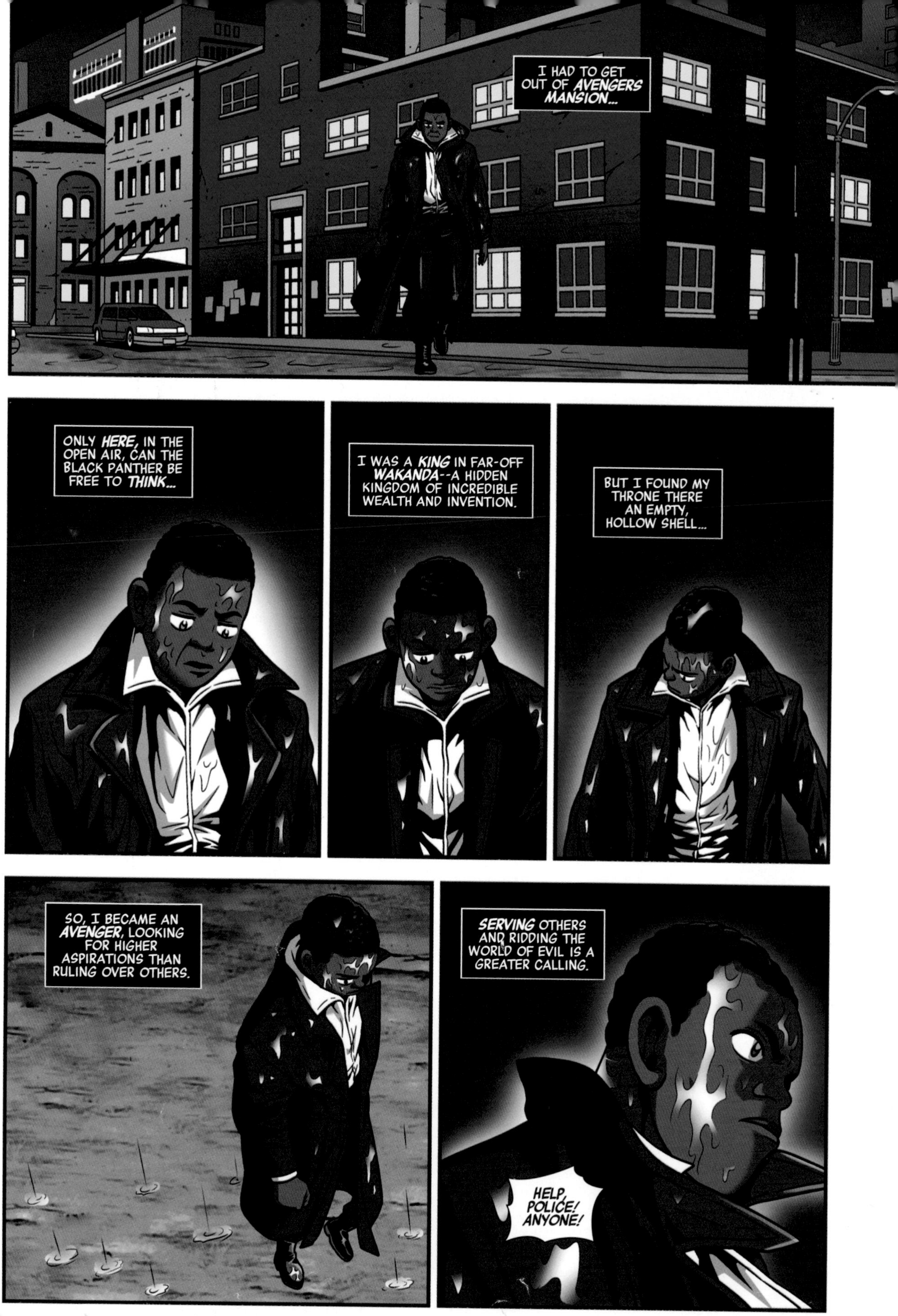
I HAD TO GET OUT OF AVENGERS MANSION...
ONLY HERE, IN THE OPEN AIR, CAN THE BLACK PANTHER BE FREE TO THINK...
I WAS A KING IN FAR-OFF WAKANDA--A HIDDEN KINGDOM OF INCREDIBLE WEALTH AND INVENTION.
BUT I FOUND MY THRONE THERE AN EMPTY, HOLLOW SHELL...
SO, I BECAME AN AVENGER, LOOKING FOR HIGHER ASPIRATIONS THAN RULING OVER OTHERS.
SERVING OTHERS AND RIDDING THE WORLD OF EVIL IS A GREATER CALLING.
HELP, POLICE! ANYONE!

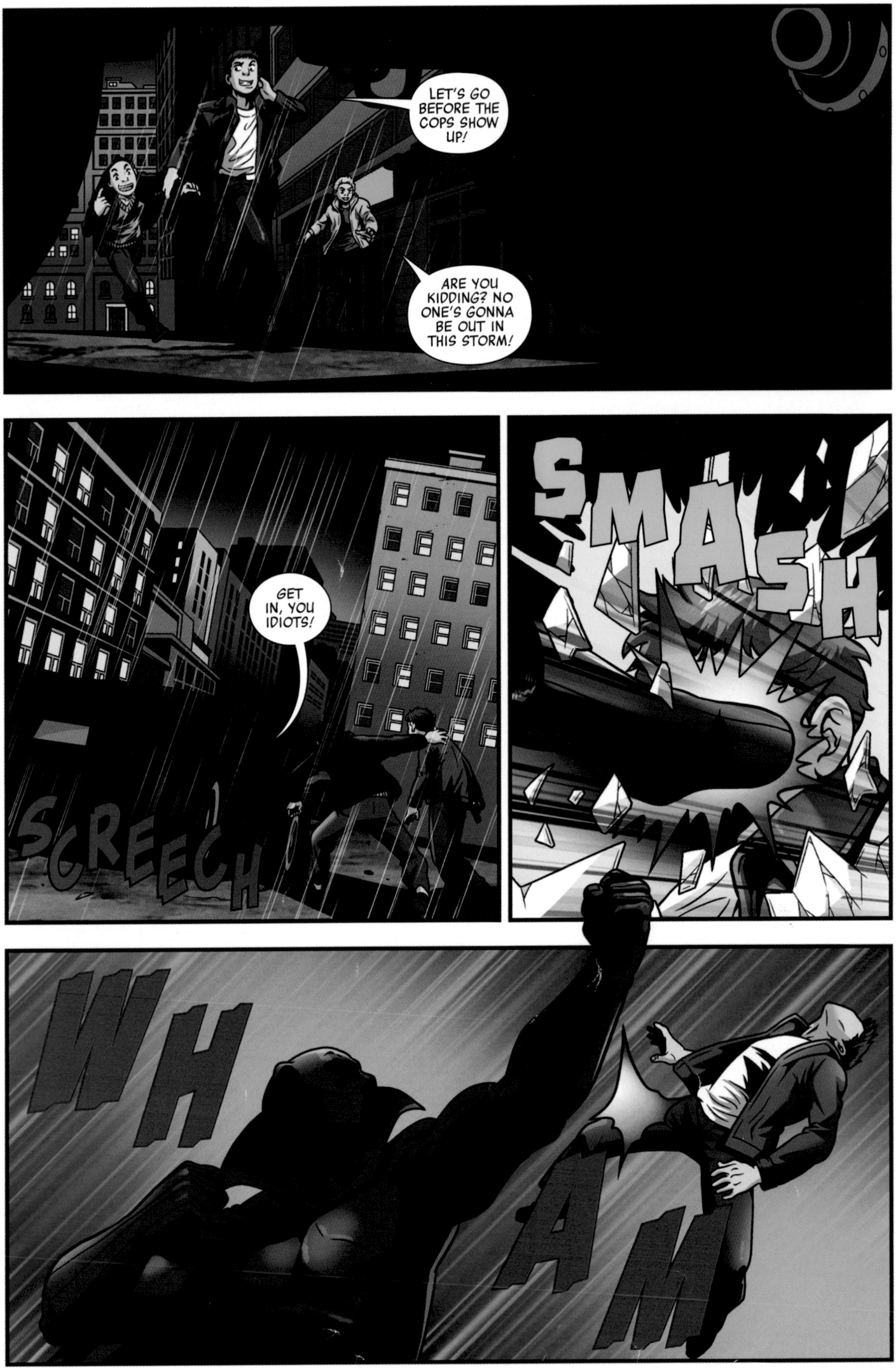
LET'S GO BEFORE THE COPS SHOW UP!
ARE YOU KIDDING? NO ONE'S GONNA BE OUT IN THIS STORM!
GET IN, YOU IDIOTS!
SCREECH
SMASH
WHAM

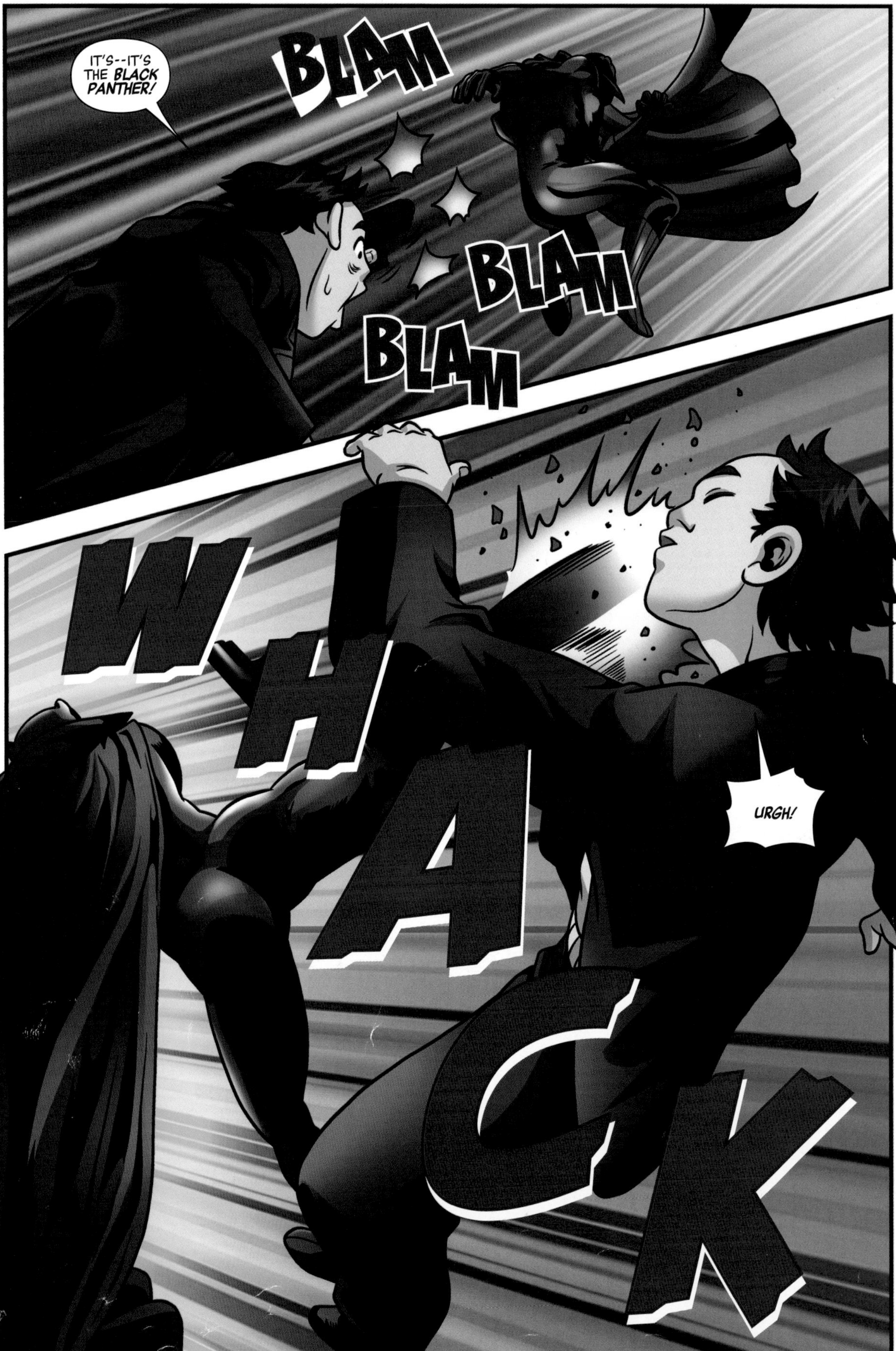
IT'S--IT'S THE BLACK PANTHER!
BLAM
BLAM
BLAM
WHACK
URGH!

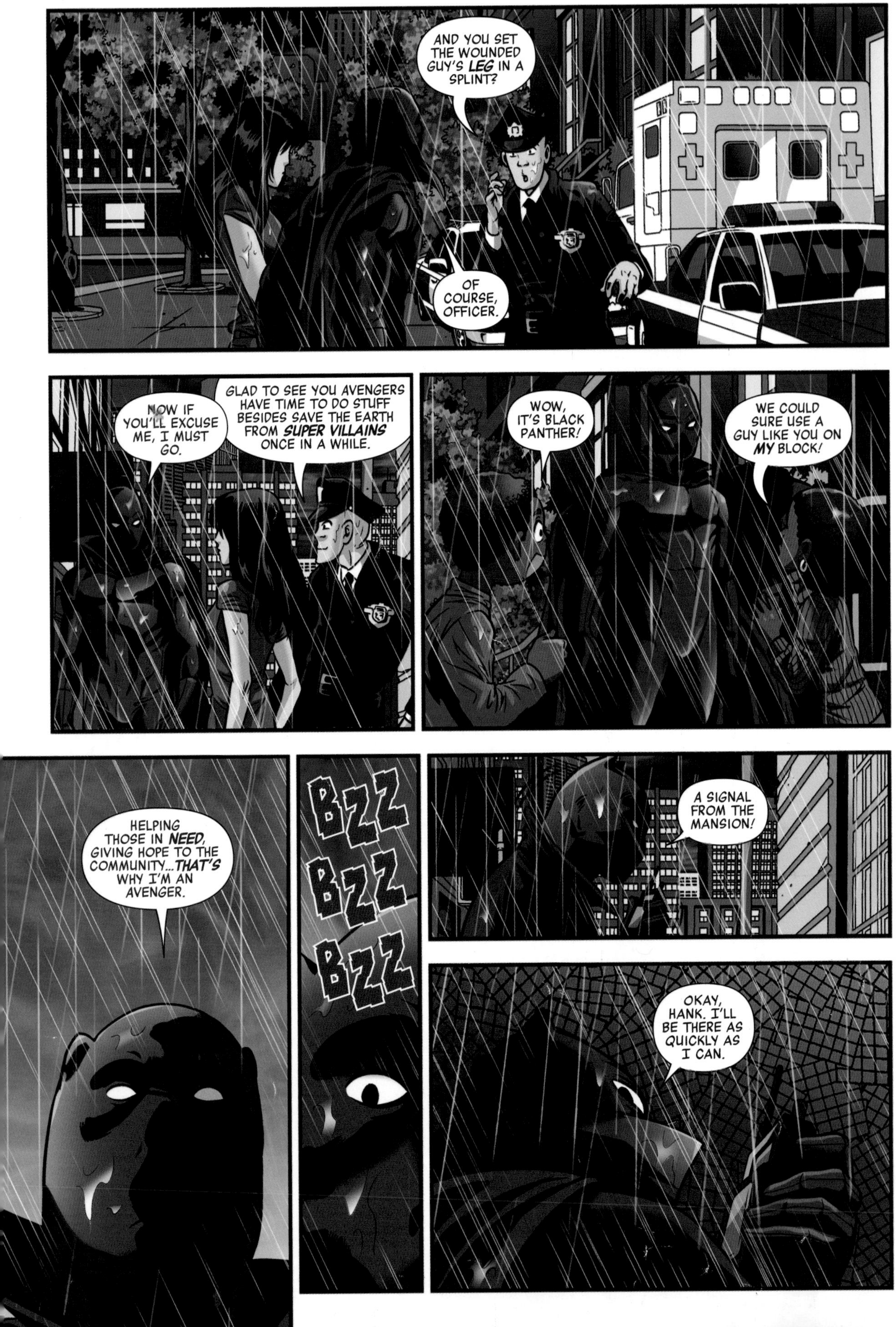
AND YOU SET THE WOUNDED GUY'S LEG IN A SPLINT?
OF COURSE, OFFICER.
GLAD TO SEE YOU AVENGERS HAVE TIME TO DO STUFF BESIDES SAVE THE EARTH FROM SUPER VILLAINS ONCE IN A WHILE.
NOW IF YOU'LL EXCUSE ME, I MUST GO.
WOW, IT'S BLACK PANTHER!
WE COULD SURE USE A GUY LIKE YOU ON MY BLOCK!
HELPING THOSE IN NEED, GIVING HOPE TO THE COMMUNITY...THAT'S WHY I'M AN AVENGER.
BZZ
BZZ
BZZ
A SIGNAL FROM THE MANSION!
OKAY, HANK. I'LL BE THERE AS QUICKLY AS I CAN.

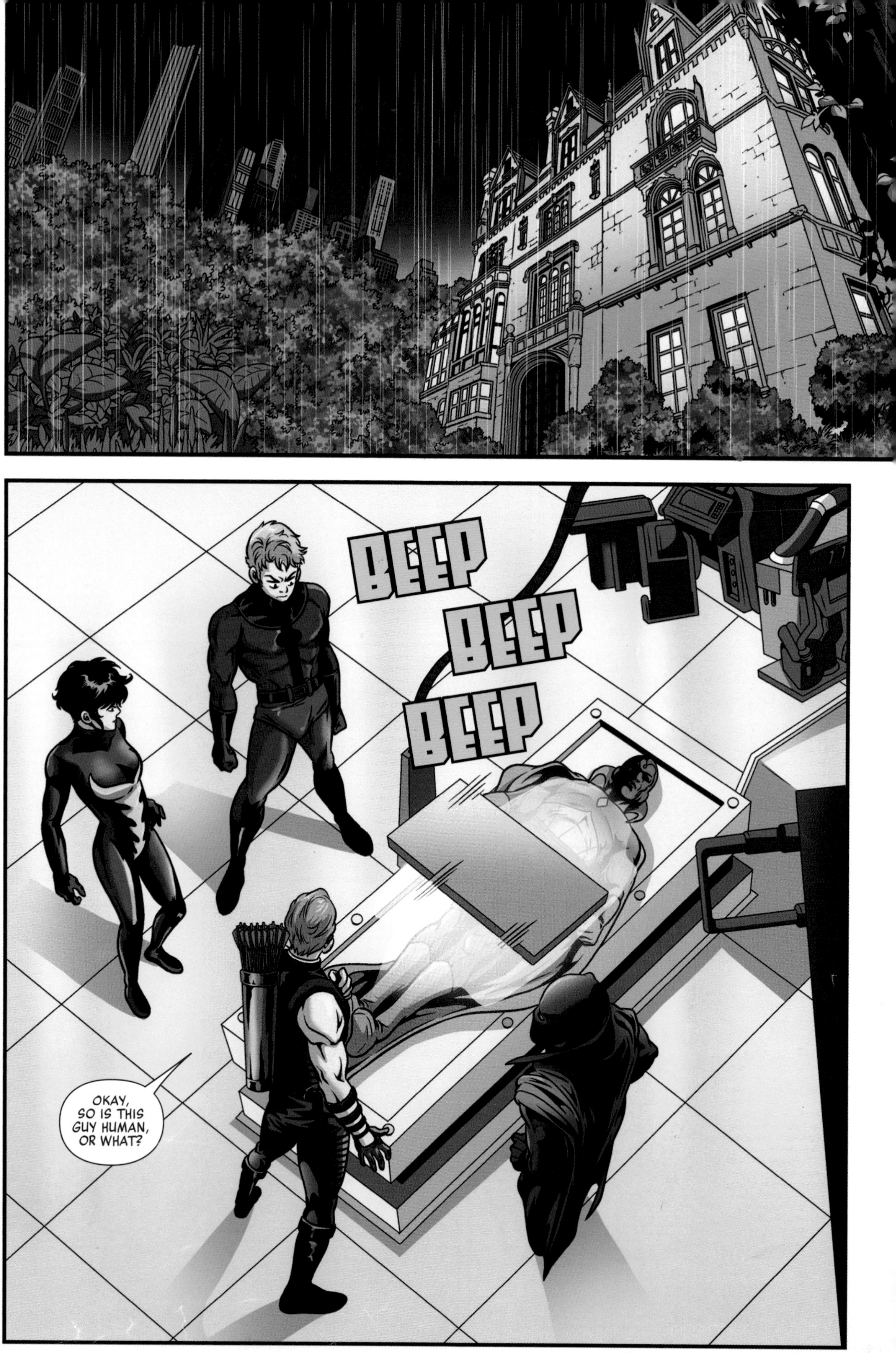
BEEP
BEEP
BEEP
OKAY, SO IS THIS GUY HUMAN, OR WHAT?

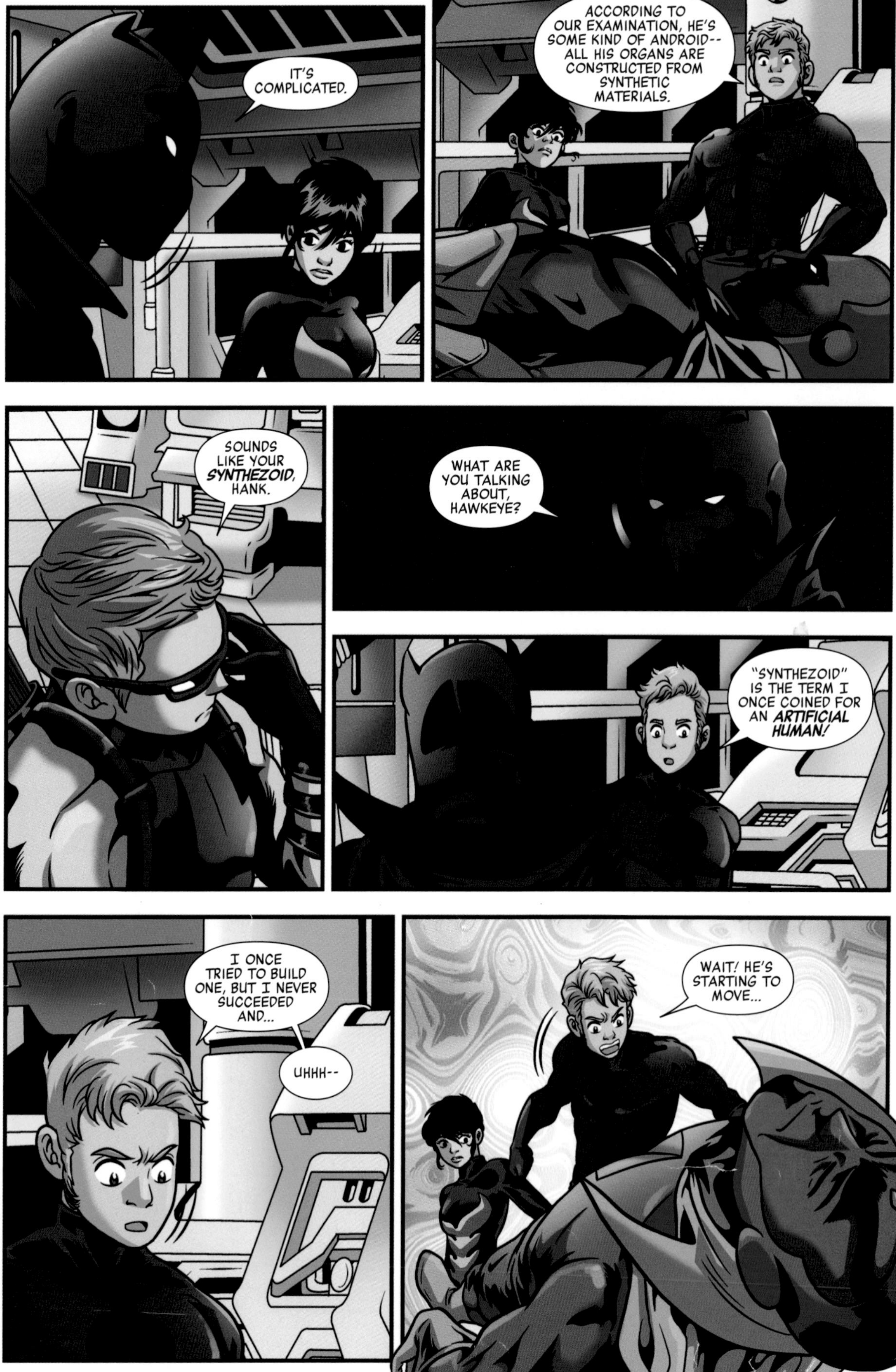
IT'S COMPLICATED.
ACCORDING TO OUR EXAMINATION, HE'S SOME KIND OF ANDROID-- ALL HIS ORGANS ARE CONSTRUCTED FROM SYNTHETIC MATERIALS.
SOUNDS LIKE YOUR SYNTHEZOID, HANK.
WHAT ARE YOU TALKING ABOUT, HAWKEYE?
"SYNTHEZOID" IS THE TERM I ONCE COINED FOR AN ARTIFICIAL HUMAN!
I ONCE TRIED TO BUILD ONE, BUT I NEVER SUCCEEDED AND...
UHHH--
WAIT! HE'S STARTING TO MOVE...

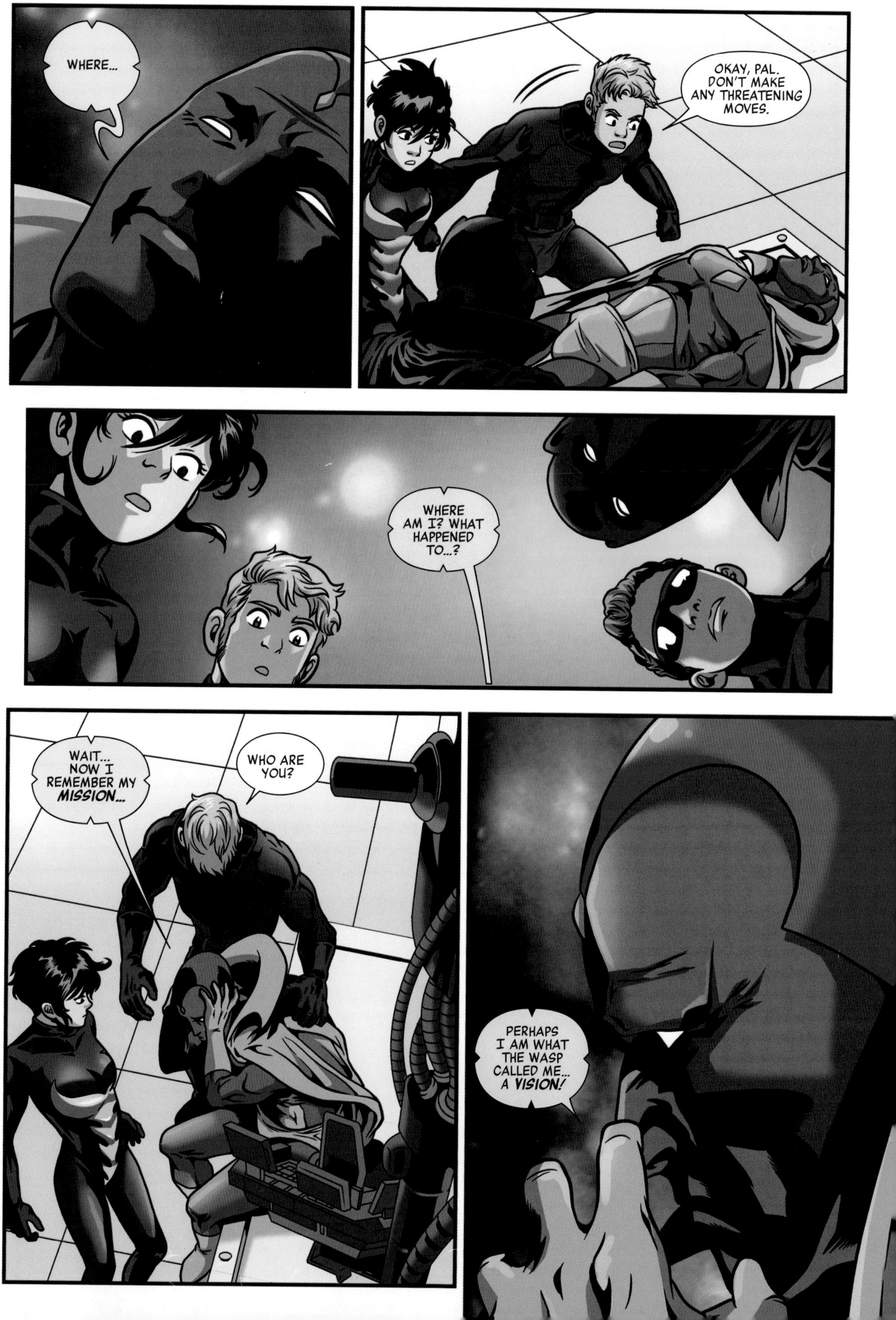
WHERE...
OKAY, PAL. DON'T MAKE ANY THREATENING MOVES.
WHERE AM I? WHAT HAPPENED TO...?
WAIT... NOW I REMEMBER MY MISSION...
WHO ARE YOU?
PERHAPS I AM WHAT THE WASP CALLED ME... A VISION!

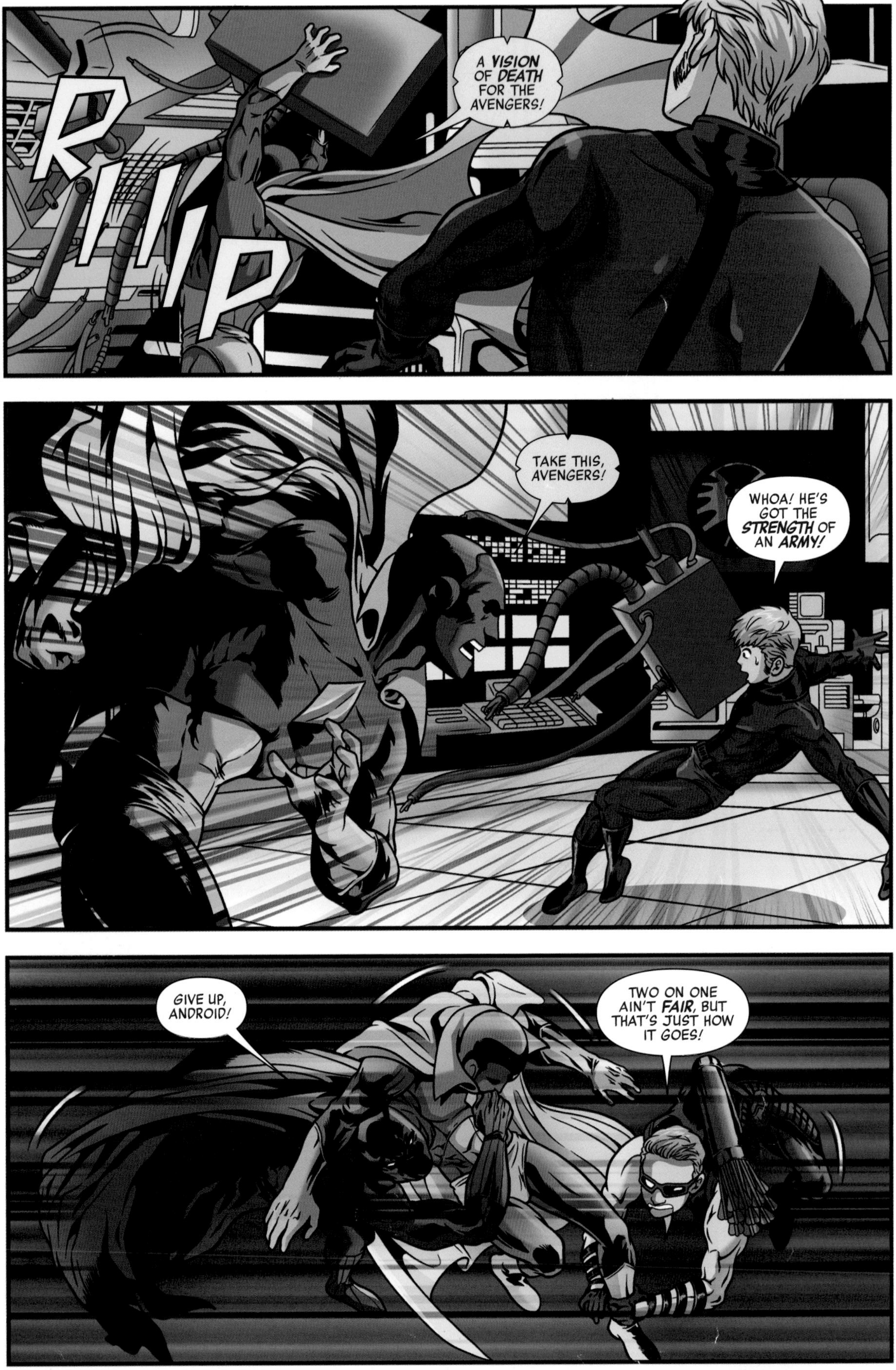
RIIIP
A VISION OF DEATH FOR THE AVENGERS!
TAKE THIS, AVENGERS!
WHOA! HE'S GOT THE STRENGTH OF AN ARMY!
GIVE UP, ANDROID!
TWO ON ONE AIN'T FAIR, BUT THAT'S JUST HOW IT GOES!

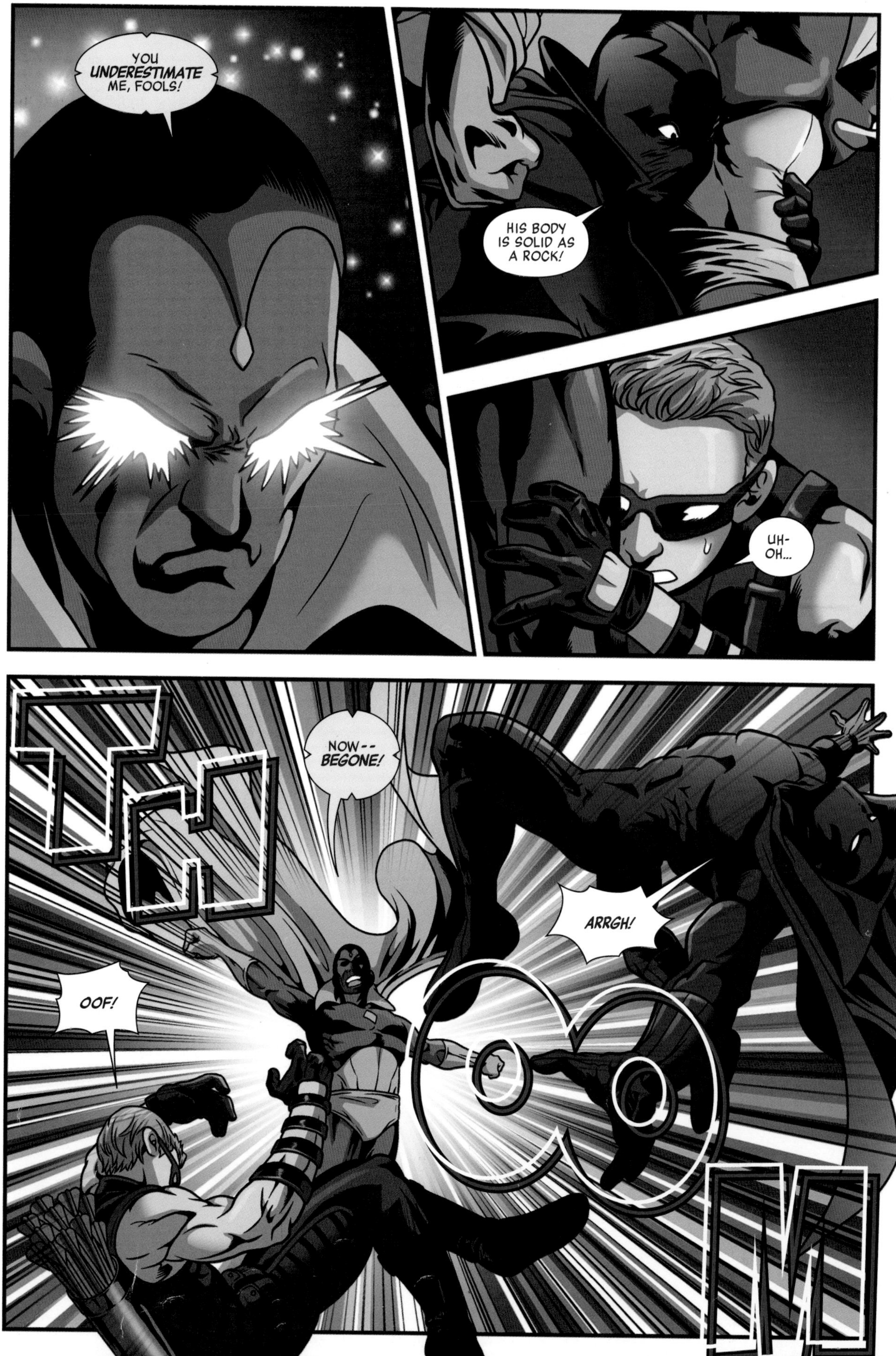

YOU UNDERESTIMATE ME, FOOLS!
HIS BODY IS SOLID AS A ROCK!
UH-OH...
NOW-- BEGONE!
THOOM
ARRGH!
OOF!

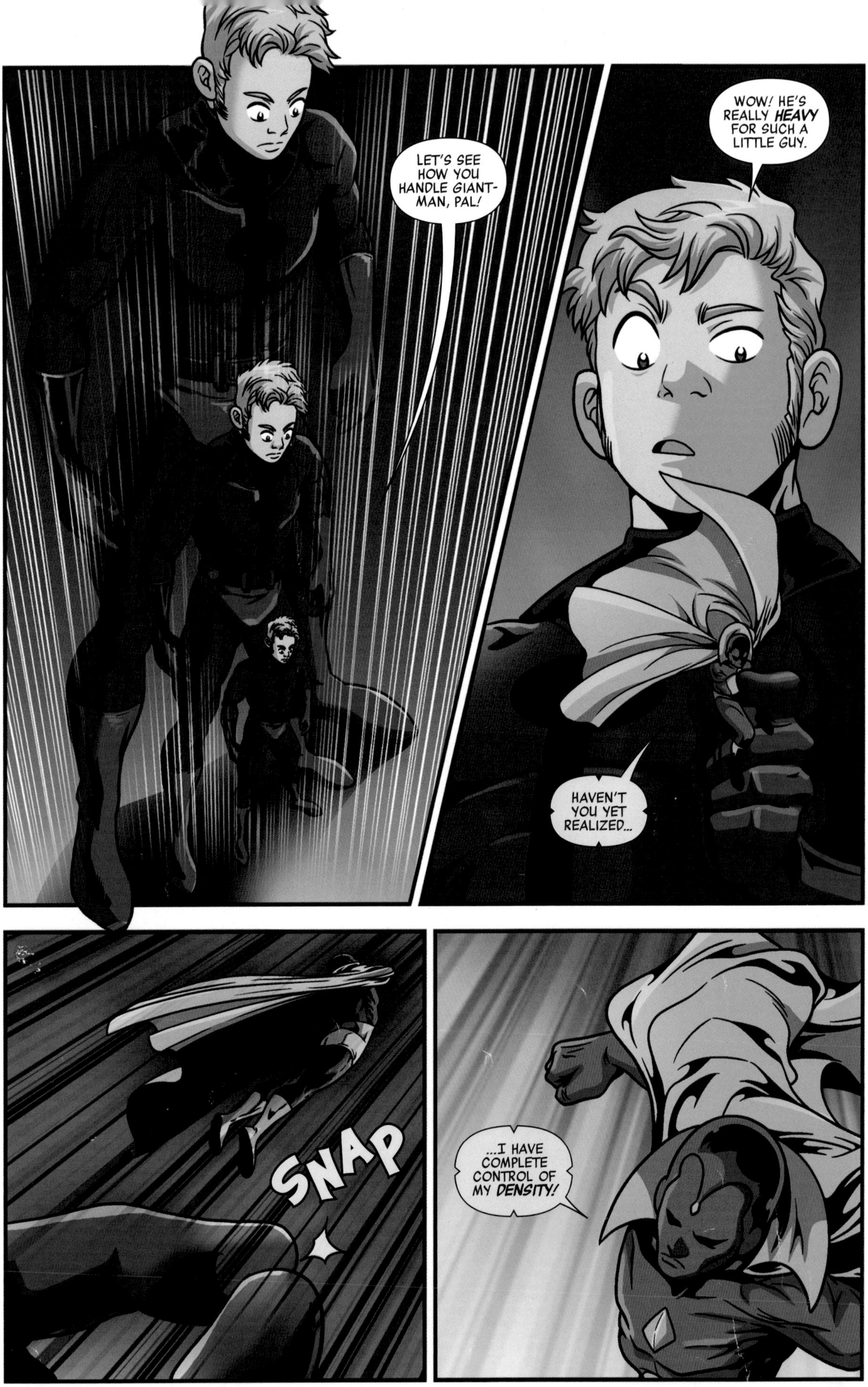
LET'S SEE HOW YOU HANDLE GIANT-MAN, PAL!
WOW! HE'S REALLY HEAVY FOR SUCH A LITTLE GUY.
HAVEN'T YOU YET REALIZED...
SNAP
...I HAVE COMPLETE CONTROL OF MY DENSITY!

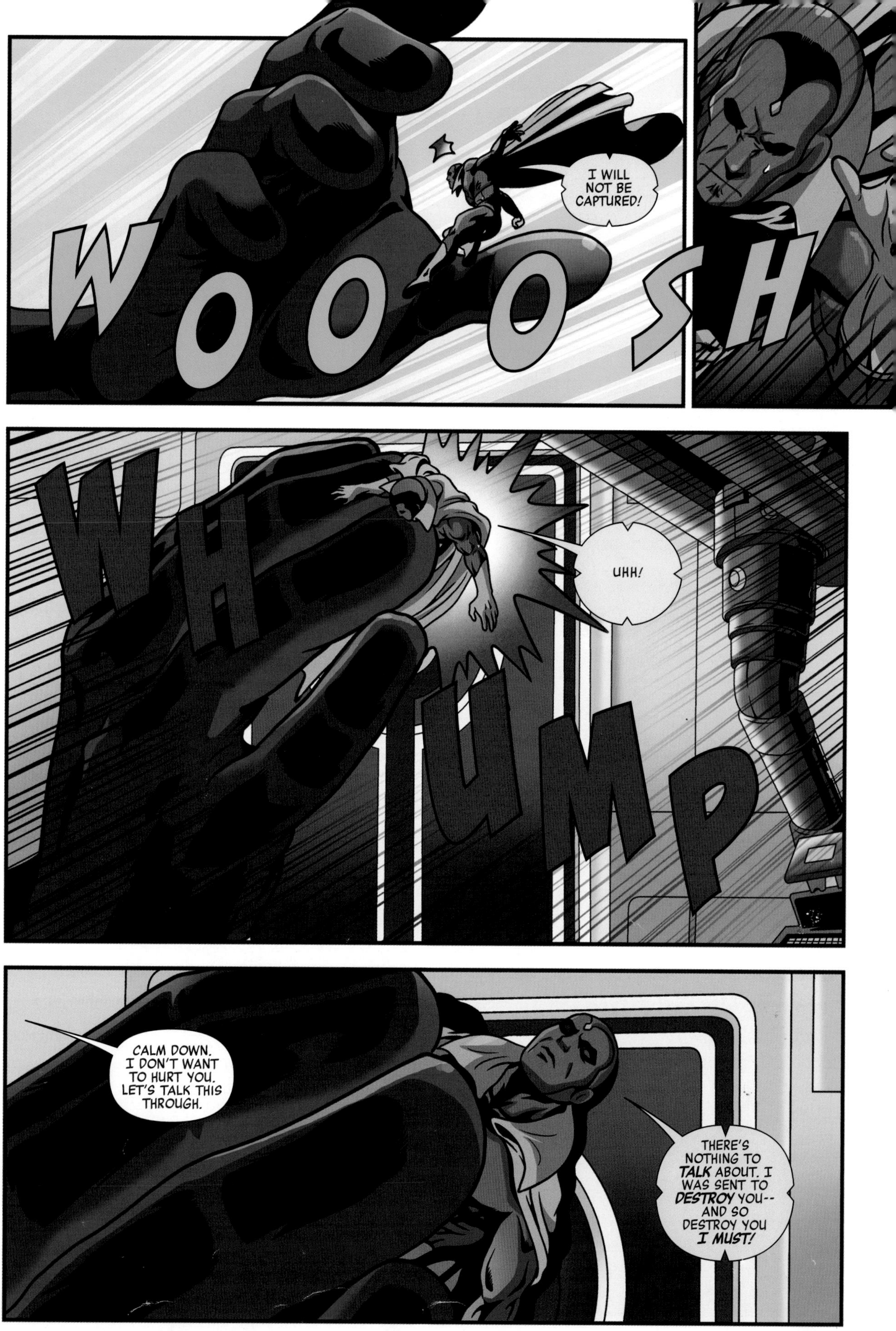
I WILL NOT BE CAPTURED!
WOOOSH
WHUMP
UHH!
CALM DOWN. I DON'T WANT TO HURT YOU. LET'S TALK THIS THROUGH.
THERE'S NOTHING TO **TALK** ABOUT. I WAS SENT TO **DESTROY** YOU-- AND SO DESTROY YOU **I MUST!**

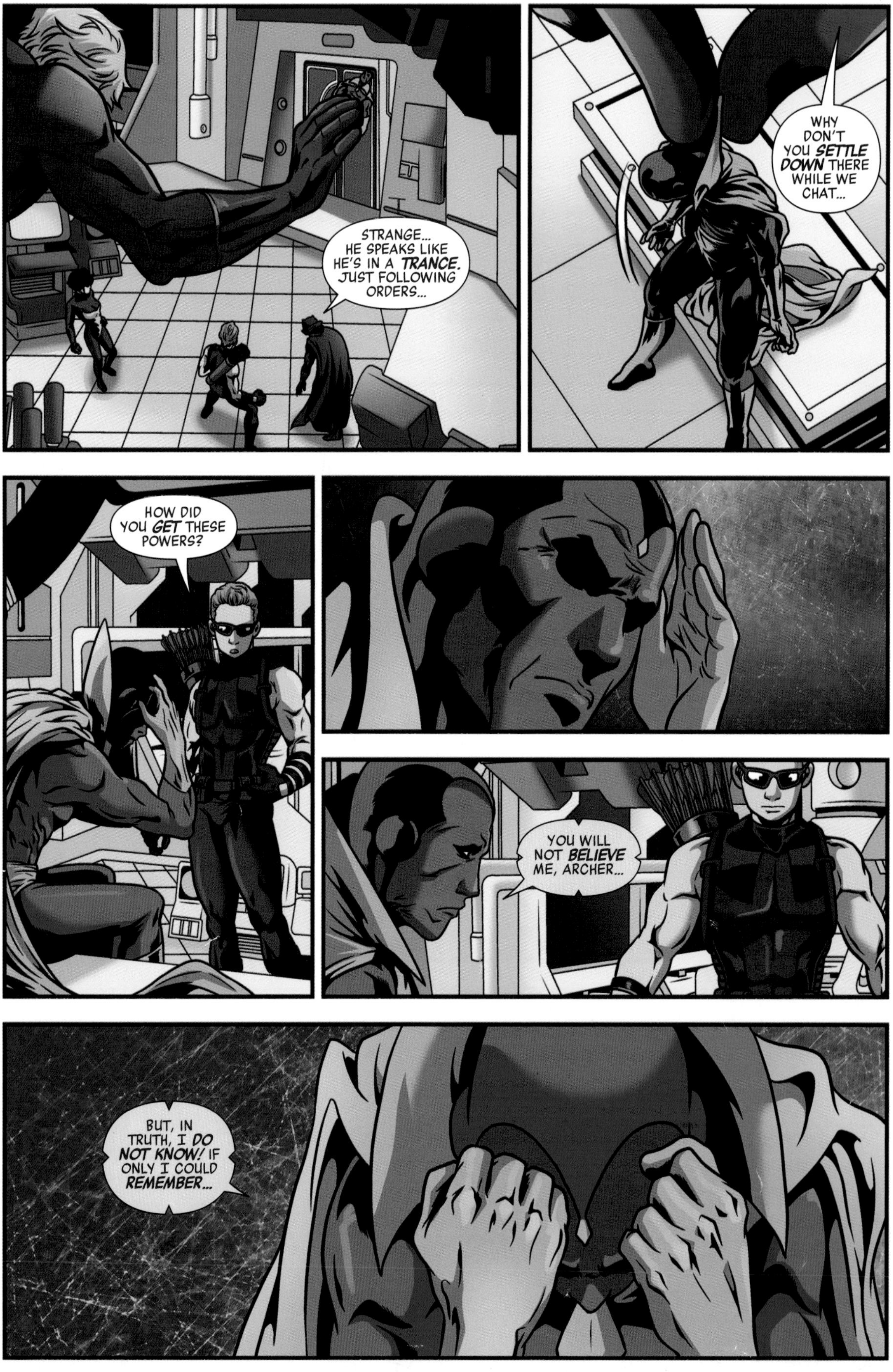
STRANGE... HE SPEAKS LIKE HE'S IN A TRANCE. JUST FOLLOWING ORDERS...
WHY DON'T YOU SETTLE DOWN THERE WHILE WE CHAT...
HOW DID YOU GET THESE POWERS?
YOU WILL NOT BELIEVE ME, ARCHER...
BUT, IN TRUTH, I DO NOT KNOW! IF ONLY I COULD REMEMBER...

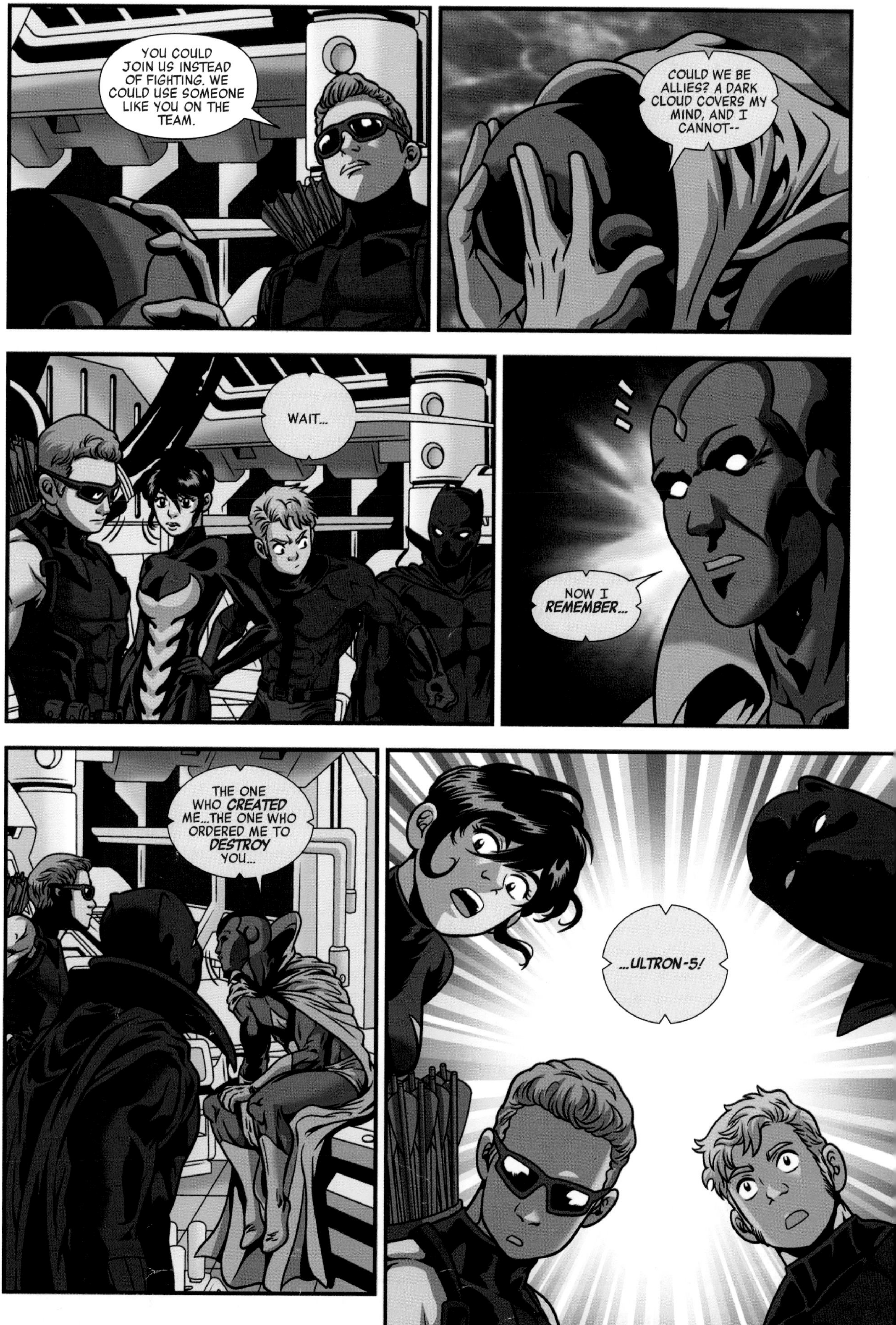
YOU COULD JOIN US INSTEAD OF FIGHTING. WE COULD USE SOMEONE LIKE YOU ON THE TEAM.
COULD WE BE ALLIES? A DARK CLOUD COVERS MY MIND, AND I CANNOT--
WAIT...
NOW I REMEMBER...
THE ONE WHO CREATED ME...THE ONE WHO ORDERED ME TO DESTROY YOU...
...ULTRON-5!

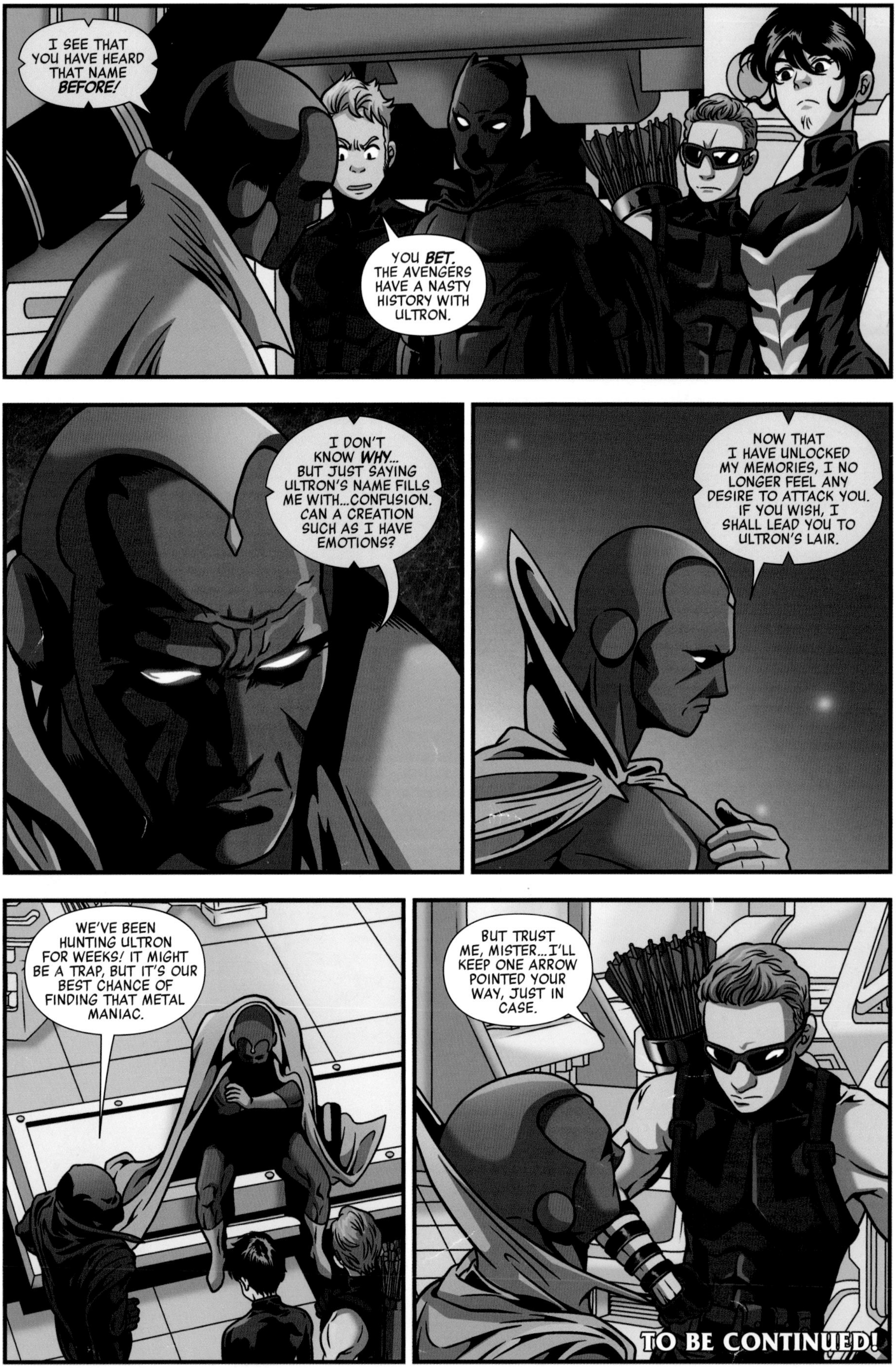
I SEE THAT YOU HAVE HEARD THAT NAME *BEFORE!*
YOU *BET.* THE AVENGERS HAVE A NASTY HISTORY WITH ULTRON.
I DON'T KNOW *WHY*... BUT JUST SAYING ULTRON'S NAME FILLS ME WITH...CONFUSION. CAN A CREATION SUCH AS I HAVE EMOTIONS?
NOW THAT I HAVE UNLOCKED MY MEMORIES, I NO LONGER FEEL ANY DESIRE TO ATTACK YOU. IF YOU WISH, I SHALL LEAD YOU TO ULTRON'S LAIR.
WE'VE BEEN HUNTING ULTRON FOR WEEKS! IT MIGHT BE A TRAP, BUT IT'S OUR BEST CHANCE OF FINDING THAT METAL MANIAC.
BUT TRUST ME, MISTER...I'LL KEEP ONE ARROW POINTED YOUR WAY, JUST IN CASE.
TO BE CONTINUED!